Instantly her ch

The raw, gravel tone of his voice scratched over every sensitive part of her body. She should have been surprised by the question, but she wasn't. It had been there, simmering between them, she'd wanted it, Santo just had the confidence to dig that deep. Her heart thundering in one powerful pump, rushing blood through her body and making her skin tingle, so much so that she felt the echoes of it reverberating around her heart while she held her breath. She bit her lip, knowing that this was a line she couldn't come back from. That the door she had opened a little was about to be pushed even further.

"No," she said, holding his intent gaze. She wanted him to see the truth. To know it. "Truth or dare?" she asked, before she could chicken out.

"Dare," he replied, sending sparks down into her core.

She closed the step between them, her heart in her throat, her pulse beating at a furious rate.

"I dare you to kiss—"

Pippa Roscoe lives in Norfolk near her family and makes daily promises to herself that this is the day she'll leave the computer to take a long walk in the countryside. She can't remember a time when she wasn't dreaming about handsome heroes and innocent heroines. Totally her mother's fault, of course—she gave Pippa her first romance to read at the age of seven! She is inconceivably happy that she gets to share those daydreams with you all. Follow her on Twitter, @pipparoscoe.

Books by Pippa Roscoe

Harlequin Presents

The Wife the Spaniard Never Forgot
His Jet-Set Nights with the Innocent
In Bed with Her Billionaire Bodyguard
Twin Consequences of That Night

The Royals of Svardia

Snowbound with His Forbidden Princess
Stolen from Her Royal Wedding
Claimed to Save His Crown

A Billion-Dollar Revenge

Expecting Her Enemy's Heir

The Greek Groom Swap

Greek's Temporary "I Do"

Visit the Author Profile page
at Harlequin.com for more titles.

FORBIDDEN UNTIL MIDNIGHT

PIPPA ROSCOE

PRESENTS

Harlequin®
PRESENTS™

ISBN-13: 978-1-335-93929-6

Forbidden Until Midnight

Recycling programs for this product may not exist in your area.

Harlequin Enterprises ULC
22 Adelaide St. West, 41st Floor
Toronto, Ontario M5H 4E3, Canada
www.Harlequin.com

Printed in Lithuania

MIX
Paper | Supporting responsible forestry
FSC® C021394

FORBIDDEN UNTIL MIDNIGHT

For Annie West.

Thank you so much for your time, your thoughts, your walks, your book recommendations and your company!

A delight and a true joy.

xx

CHAPTER ONE

New Year's Eve nine years ago, Munich

SANTO SABATINI GAZED about him with such open disdain
and barely suppressed irritation that the guests attending
the Albrechts' party were giving him at least a three-foot-
wide berth. He scowled again, shrugging into the black
tuxedo jacket he disliked intensely. Supposedly the mark
of money, Santo only associated the formal attire with
the sneering superiority that disguised the kind of wilful
ignorance and laziness that turned his stomach.

He would have turned his back on the whole sorry
affair, but for one reason. Six years ago he'd made an
unbreakable promise, a vow, and nothing and no one
would stop him from fulfilling it.

Pietro had been more like a father to him than the
bastard that had given him blood, genes and the eyes
that stared back at Santo in the mirror every day. The
only other thing he'd inherited from his father, after his
death, was the Sabatini Group.

'I don't want it.'

'You don't have a choice, mio figlio,' his mother had

said, tears streaming down a cheek still bruised from
his father's fist.

'Careful,' a feline voice warned from behind him.
'The glass you're holding so tightly could snap.'

And just like that, Santo released the white-knuckled
grip memories had tightened around the champagne
flute's thin stem. The alcohol handed to him upon ar-
rival now at an unappealing room temperature, he
paused a passing waiter and swapped the champagne
for whisky. Wiping any trace of his thoughts from his
features, he turned back to see Marie-Laure taking in
the impressive display of opulent Renaissance architecture of the Munich Residenz's Hall of Antiquities.

'The Albrechts have outdone themselves this year,'
Marie-Laure observed, unable to hide the lascivious
greed in her tone.

Santo took in the changes since he'd first met her
five years ago, the year he'd gained entry to the most
exclusive event of the financial year that neither Wall
Street nor the FTSE had heard of. The year she'd seduced him, aged eighteen, in a baroque bathroom in
Dubrovnik. A memorable event he almost wished he
could forget. *Almost.*

Her dyed red hair had taken on more of a brittle as-
pect but, no matter how she behaved, it was undeniable that Marie-Laure Gerber was a startlingly beautiful
woman who wore her sensuality like both a weapon and
a shield. And while it hadn't been his first sexual experience, it had been ironically his most honest. Proved
perfectly by the way she had ruthlessly ignored him the
following year.

But it would be wrong to mistake Marie-Laure as simply the lonely widow of one of Switzerland's richest financiers. There was a reason the blundering, bulbous man had reached such dizzying heights before his death; his wife was sharper than honed steel and just as dangerous.

'Tell me, *tesorina*, what has your claws out so early this evening?' Santo asked.

The delighted peal of her laugh was as fake as his term of endearment had been.

'Rumour has it that Edward Carson's precious princess of a daughter is making her first appearance.'

Santo's gut clenched instinctively, but only bland indifference marked his features. 'Is she?'

Marie-Laure cut a side glance at him, her eyebrow raised. 'They say she is absolutely exquisite.'

Santo gave a shrug of his shoulder. 'Not my type,' he dismissed.

'They all say that. *At first.*' Marie-Laure's tone took on a diamond-hard edge, before she turned to look out across the hall. 'The children have been talking of nothing else all evening.'

Santo looked over to where the progeny of the twelve families in attendance had gathered. Or, more accurately, eleven families. He was the last and only descendant of the Sabatinis. And it would remain that way too, he swore.

The group of young twenty-somethings were the heirs of the elite. They would grow up to become the wealth of Europe, the decision-makers of millions. And each and every one of them was a spoilt brat with absolutely no idea of what hard work was.

'You think I pay even the slightest bit of notice to what they say?' he asked.

'No,' she said, turning back to Santo fully. 'You don't. It's why I like you so much.'

'You only like cold, sharp, shiny things,' he dismissed.

'Exactly,' she said, patting his chest just above his heart, and left him to stand staring at the group of young men and women whispering and gossiping, a few daring to send a glance his way once in a while.

With barely veiled scorn, he turned back to the gold-embossed display of Renaissance architecture and artwork covering every inch of the large hall. It was gaudy, it was impressive, awesome in the traditional sense of the word and, as much as he disliked every single bit of it, he respected the history of it, he respected *history*. He had to, in order not to repeat it.

Munich was as beautiful as Helsinki had been the year before and Stockholm had been the year before that. Each New Year's Eve celebration was held in a different European city, by a different family. But Marie-Laure was right; the Albrechts *had* outdone themselves this year.

No one outside of the twelve families knew of, or even heard of, what happened here. And not because it was some bacchanalian event shrouded in generations of inherited wealth, hidden behind secret handshakes or cult-like devotion. Even though, deep down, Santo had expected as much the first time he'd attended the event.

No, what happened every year on the thirty-first of December, in a different European city, hosted by each different family, was simply this: the exchange and investment of money for *more* money.

In essence it was a financial cabal and he hated every single person here. Because they would do anything in order to protect their own financial security, including turning a blind eye to violence and abuse. The exclusivity of this group of people ensured the containment of inconceivable wealth. And it wasn't lost on him that while Pietro was one of the best men he'd ever met, as the son of an ex-Mafia enforcer he would never be allowed within these hallowed halls, despite the fact that the people here were probably even bigger criminals. No, what mattered nearly as much as the zeros in your bank account to these people was genetics. And those two things made nearly every single person here almost pathologically selfish. And Santo Sabatini knew firsthand just how dangerous that could be.

He swallowed a mouthful of his whisky as the hum of whispers grew louder.

'She's here,' he was just able to make out from the buzz.

Refusing to turn, to succumb to the desire to see her finally, in the flesh, take her place as Edward Carson's heir, Santo instead remembered the words his mentor had said to him.

'It's not easy what I'm asking you. It's the longest game you'll ever play,' Pietro had warned. *'It may even take years. What I'm asking you is a lifelong commitment, so think carefully before you agree.'*

Santo hadn't needed time. He didn't doubt what the older man was saying. He understood what he was being asked. He understood that it was a secret that must be kept from everyone. Because it could dramatically change the course of a young woman's life. But the answer was easy, all the same. After everything Pietro had done for his mother, for *him*, Santo would give his all to whatever was asked. Even if that meant maintaining his connection to this hideous group of people.

So now, as Eleanor Carson finally emerged into the Hall of Antiquities of the Munich Residenz on New Year's Eve, the day after her eighteenth birthday, Santo Sabatini prepared to make good on that promise.

'Look after her, Santo. Protect *her.'*

'I will.'

Eleanor Carson gasped the moment she entered the grand hall. She had *never* seen anything more beautiful in her entire life. Her heart beat so strongly it pressed her chest against the tight bustline of her gold dress.

She had waited years for this moment. *Years.*

And now she thought she might actually explode with happiness. Eleanor looked at her father, the sparkle in his eyes, the joy on his beloved features, and knew that he was as happy for her as she was. She reached for his hand and squeezed, as he nodded for her to go to join her friends. Throughout all the beautiful and gorgeous celebrations that she'd had yesterday, *this* had been her real birthday present. She cast a glance back at her mother, something in her gaze catching Eleanor just a little strangely, before it was masked with a smile.

'Go on,' her mother said with a kind laugh, and that was all the permission Eleanor needed before she searched out Dilly from amongst the crowd of familiar faces. Friends of the family, school friends from a few years above, the circles she moved in had been tight knit but, now she was eighteen years old, finally, she got to join them *here*.

Until this moment, the New Year's Eve parties were known only to Eleanor through rumours and whispers. No one dared speak of what happened here, but the vague details and hints only increased her curiosity to fever pitch. In her mind it had become a fairy tale ball fit for a princess, and looking around the Hall of Antiquities, it was beyond her wildest imagination.

Gold, pale blue, dusky pink and alabaster filled the periphery of her vision, the gentle hum of chatter overlaying the pretty strains from a live orchestra hidden from view. Shivers of absolute joy rippled across her skin and her chest felt as full as if she'd held her breath for an eternity just to be here.

'Lee!' she heard Dilly cry from part way across the room and couldn't help but laugh at the friend she hadn't seen since she'd graduated a year earlier than Eleanor, last July.

'Oh, I am *so* glad to see you,' Eleanor said, allowing herself to be swept up in Dilly's warm embrace.

'Me too! It has been positively *dull* here without you,' Dilly confided. 'You look absolutely delicious—all the boys are having *conniptions*.'

Eleanor batted at her friend's arm. 'Don't be silly.'

'I'm not!' Dilly cried, before tucking her hand into

the curve of her arm. 'Come, let me give you the tour,' she said, pulling Eleanor towards the far end of the hall. 'The Albrechts are hosting this year. Next year, it's going to be the Pichlers in Vienna, which will be equally, if not *more*, impressive than this,' Dilly confided.

Eleanor didn't think it could get even better than this, but kept that to herself.

'And how are the family? Mater and Pater?'

'They're good,' Eleanor said with a smile, and remembered her younger brother's sulking frown as they'd left him in the hotel before his bedtime.

'But I want to come with you.'

'Not until you're eighteen, like Ellie,' her father had said.

'I'll say. Your father's just done a spectacular deal with the Müllers, he should be on cloud nine,' exclaimed Dilly.

'They celebrated all last night,' Eleanor confirmed, with a secret thread of pride. She'd spent weeks listening to her father negotiate the deal, her nails almost bitten to the quick, because she had suggested the deal. Oh, she wasn't naïve, she knew that her father would never do anything he didn't want to do, but she *had* suggested it. And he had thought it was a good idea. And secretly she hoped that would help him begin to see that she really did want to study business at university. That she wanted to follow in his footsteps one day. Oh, the business would be passed to Freddie, she knew that. But... she might be able to be a part of that business too.

They came to the far end of the incredible hall and turned, so that the entire room was on display.

'Okay,' Dilly announced. 'As you know, no one from outside the families are allowed. It's the one night of the year where everyone can just be themselves without worrying about political enemies or financial repercussions.'

Eleanor nodded. The impossible exclusivity and secrecy surrounding the New Year's Eve gatherings had always been what had made her want to attend so much.

'Now, over by the tables, you should probably be able to recognise some familiar faces.'

Eleanor's gaze found a pair of deep brown eyes joining with hers, under a mop of rich blond hair and lips that had curved into a smile. Her heart beat just a little quicker, recognising Antony Fairchild.

'Of course, you know Tony already.'

'I wouldn't say I *know* him,' Eleanor confessed.

'Looks like he knows you though,' Dilly teased with a nudge of her shoulder.

Eleanor felt her cheeks pink under the older boy's perusal. He'd been a few years ahead of her at Sandrilling—the boarding school on the outskirts of London that many of the children of the families gathered here had attended. She'd not thought that he'd even known her name, but the way he was still looking at her made her heart trip over itself.

Unable to stop an answering smile from curving her own mouth, she allowed Dilly to pull her attention back with a roll of her eyes.

'Smitten already?' Dilly asked.

'I have no idea what you're talking about,' she replied, a wry smile on her lips.

Eleanor looked across the hall and from amongst the
nearly two hundred people gathered in the glorious hall
found her parents talking to the Fairchilds, her mother
looking a little distracted. Unease twisted in Eleanor's
gut. Her mother hadn't wanted her to come tonight, but
Eleanor didn't know why. For years, all Eleanor had
wanted was to be a part of this. To be part of the world
her parents kept hidden from her. The glamour, the exclusivity, the *secrecy*... Being here meant they trusted
her with that and it was as much a signifier of adult-
hood as her eighteenth birthday. Now her life could *really* begin.

Dilly was distracted by something over Eleanor's
shoulder. 'Give me two secs? I'll be right back.'

Eleanor didn't mind one bit. She'd actually been hoping for a moment to herself, just to take it all in. It was
so much *more* than she'd expected. The noise was quite
something from a crowd of nearly two hundred or so
guests. A couple passed in front of her, forcing her to
take a step back out of the way and to bump up against
something hard.

Someone.

'I'm so sorry,' she said, turning to see who she'd
crashed into.

Horror filled her as she took in the sight of a dark-
haired man staring down at the amber stain soaking
into his white shirt.

'Oh, no, I'm so sorry!' she exclaimed, reaching
quickly for some napkins on the side table beside them
and pressing them against the spilled alcohol in the hope
of limiting the damage.

The moment that her hand met his chest the man moved back, his arms raised, as if to avoid any possible contact with her. But no matter the distance, the simmering anger in the man's gaze was palpable.

She bit her lips together and raised her eyes from the man's chest to his face and then stopped. Everything stopped. The brief flick of the man's gaze to hers and then back to his shirt was all it had taken to strike her still.

Rich, dark, sumptuous curling hair covered a head that was bent to stare down at his now ruined shirt. But even then, she could tell that he was nearly a foot taller than her in her heels. The sharp lines of his cheekbones and patrician nose led her gaze down to near cruelly sensual lips that sent a shiver down her spine. A delicious one.

But it was the bright aquamarine of his eyes that struck her hardest. They were unexpected, against the clear Mediterranean stamp of his heritage. Greece maybe, Italy more likely. She was caught staring when he looked up and held her gaze when most would have looked away. *She* should have looked away. She would have, but for the moment when she thought that she saw something other than disdain in his gaze, but then he snatched the napkins from the hand that had dropped to her side and dabbed ineffectually at his ruined shirt.

'I really am—'

'Sorry, yes. I heard you the first time. And the second.'

Shame and embarrassment coloured her cheeks a hot

pink. She felt gauche, foolish and a little childish next to this man.

But that was no excuse for bad manners. Shaking herself out of it, she put on her best smile and held out her hand.

'Eleanor Carson,' she said by way of introduction.

Santo hadn't intended to actually have to speak to her. He'd thought, naïvely perhaps, that he might be able to keep watch over her from afar. So this awkward exchange had certainly not been a part of his plans.

As she stared up at him, her face strangely determined, he took a moment to take in the 'exquisite' Eleanor Carson. Oh, he could understand what had got the younger generation's knickers in a twist. Eleanor Carson would grow up to be quite a beautiful young woman, he was sure. Dark hair swept back stylishly from skin as pale as milk. Her eyes, a deep brown, were almost infuriatingly innocent. An innocence he'd never had the luxury of.

Her dress made the most of it, of course. Never one to be particularly interested in women's fashion, other than when he was taking it off his chosen companion, he supposed it suited her. Little puff sleeves capped her shoulders…his eyes skimming over a simple neckline and a corseted top…before flaring out into wide skirts, the entire thing made of a golden material that made him think of long-forgotten fairy tales.

But he had stared too long and just as he held out his hand, hers dropped away. He bit his teeth together, intensely disliking the awkwardness of the entire encounter, and waited. Belatedly recovering herself, she met his hand with her fingers, which left him fairly sure that the Carson girl was disappointingly insipid.

'Isn't it just incredible?' she asked, full of a wholly unwarranted exuberance.

He stared at her blankly, her observation only more evidence against her.

'It's my first time here,' she confided, pressing on despite his clear disinclination to pursue this conversation. He wondered absently what other inane observation she might be capable of, and looked away when she blushed beneath his scrutiny.

'Would never have known,' he uttered beneath his breath, snagging a fresh glass of whisky from a passing waiter, more than a little frustrated that he would spend the rest of the night smelling like a distillery.

Before the waiter could disappear, Eleanor beckoned him over and whispered something in the young man's ear. The eagerness of the boy—probably the same age as her—was almost pitiful. He nodded and rushed off.

She'd probably ordered some frothy cocktail that disguised any offending taste of alcohol.

He opened his mouth to make an excuse to leave, but Eleanor pushed on determinedly.

'I've not been to Munich before. I'm hoping that there will be some time to see it before we leave, the day after tomorrow. Have you? Are there any attractions you could suggest?'

He turned back to face her full on, with a raised eyebrow that was *sure* to convey his disbelief that she would actually be asking him for tourist spot recommendations.

Once again, he attempted to excuse himself.

'Because, honestly,' she pressed on, not giving him the chance, 'I quite like looking around cities when they're quiet. It's as if you get to see something that no one else does. And tomorrow, I'd imagine most people will be still in bed, or nursing a hangover so...'

She trailed off, having seen something while Santo was still trying to make sense of the image he now had of Eleanor wandering along isolated streets just before sunrise.

'Oh, thank you,' she said to the waiter, who had returned and passed her a bag before leaving.

Eleanor turned back to Santo. 'This is for you. It should fit. It obviously won't be as nice as the one I ruined, but at least it won't be stained. Or smell,' she added with a smile that was near delightful. She bobbed her head, wished him a good rest of the evening and disappeared, leaving him holding a bag with a cellophane-wrapped white shirt, quite unsure as to what had just happened.

'Wait,' he called before he could stop himself.

She turned back, just a few feet from where he stood, a small smile on her face. It was a Mona Lisa smile— not fake or forced, but as if she knew she'd surprised him. Because he hadn't thought her capable of the kind of awareness that was required not only to recompense him for the damage to his shirt, but more than that, to do it in such a way that it had been subtle, seamless. Anyone else here would have simply shrugged it off and left him to it.

'Santo Sabatini,' he offered.

'Nice to meet you, Mr Sabatini,' she said, a broad, almost beautiful, smile stretching across her features, before disappearing into the crowd, leaving a feeling turning in his chest that lasted for much longer than Santo was comfortable with.

As Eleanor made her way back to Dilly and the group she was with, she couldn't help but feel a fizz of excitement humming through her veins. She cast a quick glance over her shoulder to where Santo Sabatini— Italian, most definitely—was *still* staring after her. Her heart fluttered a little. It had hardly been anything, but something about surprising him had pleased her.

She risked another glance, but this time he was gone, and that pleasure dimmed just a bit. Dilly welcomed her back into the group and pulled her to her side, next to Tony Fairchild. Eleanor smiled shyly at him when he turned to make room for her.

He caught her up on the conversation, an argument about whether one of the boys in the group should invest with another. Eleanor let the conversation flow around them until there was a lull.

'Dilly, what do you know about Santo Sabatini?'

She wrinkled her nose. 'Best to stay away from him. His father died about six years ago and the ugly rumours are that Santo was *there*.'

The way that Dilly said 'there' seemed to imply *involved* rather than *present*, and Eleanor found herself frowning at the thought. Had she got it so wrong? Was Santo Sabatini actually dangerous? She didn't think she'd felt that he was.

'But he inherited the Sabatini Group—the biggest privately held company in Italy—at just eighteen and even though some of the families tried to group together to buy it from him, he refused.'

'He's a pompous git,' Tony added. Eleanor started just a little, not aware he'd been listening to their conversation. But he caught her gaze and rolled his eyes in a joking way, becoming the handsome, charming rake she remembered from school. He closed the distance between them to say, 'But don't mind him. He doesn't usually bother us much.'

Eleanor nodded eagerly as he took her arm and pulled her to his side, and when he smiled at her she felt a little flutter and thought that she was the luckiest girl here.

And by the time the clock struck midnight she'd forgotten all thoughts of the tall, brooding Italian and believed that perhaps, just like the fairy tales she'd loved so much, she had met her very own Prince Charming in Antony Fairchild. And the way that his eyes sparkled at her, she began to hope that it was more than just a fantasy.

CHAPTER TWO

New Year's Eve eight years ago, Vienna

WHAT A DIFFERENCE a year made, Eleanor thought as she emerged into the air-controlled environment of the Pichlers' wine cellars with a diamond ring on her finger and a fiancé on her arm.

Antony smiled at her, the not-so-subtle heat in his gaze making her heart flutter in excitement. Any hesitation she might have had about the fast-paced progression of their relationship had disintegrated beneath her father's exuberant encouragement three months ago.

The proposal had been nothing short of extravagant, Tony whisking her away for a few nights in a luxurious cabin in the Lyngen Alps, north of the Arctic Circle in Norway. Before the Northern lights, he'd told her that she was more beautiful to him, more precious, and he could never want or think of anyone else ever again.

She wasn't as naïve as some people thought. She *did* understand that her relationship with Tony benefited both businesses and families. Her knowledge of her father's company was enough to make that painstakingly clear, and if it hadn't been already then the whispers that such a connection in the group had never happened before would have made it doubly so.

But life had been a whirlwind ever since the last New Year's Eve party. They'd been almost inseparable since that night. Bouquets of red roses and white lilies had arrived the following day and within weeks she had been whisked away on a romantic trip to Paris. Date by date, each one increasingly extravagant, Tony had teased from her the future that she wanted—a family, just like her own, the importance of the family business, the tenets by which she had been raised, that she wanted to continue. And she'd been thrilled to discover that he wanted the same.

Impassioned declarations of love had made her feel special—desired and loved in equal measure. And if her mother had urged caution then her father's eager acceptance had swept any concerns aside and Eleanor had fallen head over heels for Tony's charm and his easy-going nature. She could see it, the lives they would make, familiar and comfortable, solid and successful. It would make her father so happy.

'I'm going to get us a drink,' Tony whispered in her ear, pressing a light kiss to the sensitive flesh just beneath, sending a shiver of delight across her body.

She'd been worried about asking him to *wait* until they were married, wanting her first time to be special, with the person she loved and trusted most in this world. But he had assured her that he wanted her only to be comfortable and happy. But recently she'd been regretting that decision. Maybe she didn't need to wait until she was married, she thought as he disappeared into the crowd filling the space under the low arched brick walls and ceilings of the Pichlers' underground wine cellars.

She'd been wrong to think that they would be dark and grimy, because the cellars were actually beautifully lit with carefully controlled temperatures. Racks of wine bottles were displayed behind gleaming glass and she felt as if she were in a gallery. The large wine cabinets created little nooks and corners that were already filling with people dressed in jewels and silks, all glittering in the festive atmosphere.

'Nineteen years old and engaged to one of England's finest bachelors—who would have thought it?' Dilly mused as she pulled Eleanor into a warm embrace and out of her thoughts.

'Yes, congratulations,' added Ekaterina Kivi, who had attended Sandrilling in the year ahead of her.

Eleanor smiled happily at the redhead. 'Thank you,' she said sincerely. 'I honestly never thought I could be this happy,' she confessed as she caught her father's proud eye from across the room.

'I bet Daddy is happy,' Dilly said, leaning into her shoulder. 'Barely a year out of school and you're already set for life.'

Eleanor's smile dimmed a little at the way Dilly made it sound as if her life was over. As if there was nothing else to achieve now that she had a fiancé.

Yes, Tony had talked her into taking another year off from university to help host several incredibly important dinners, as he tried to cement his place in his father's investment company. But she had enjoyed doing it, and doing it well. She hadn't found it difficult at all, following her mother's lead after so many years.

And no, she might not have liked keeping her opinions on their conversations about business to herself after Tony had laughed, excusing her enthusiasm, when she'd disagreed with one of his guests. But she knew what kind of pressure he was under. She'd seen that too, from her father. And she'd always wanted what her parents had. The perfect marriage, the love and the security. It had been what she'd wanted as a child and it was what she wanted now.

So she would happily accept the little adjustments to her life until they settled down and she could return her focus to her studies. Because she *did* have dreams for herself. Even if they were going to have to wait a little while.

'Well, I'm sure that you will be blissfully happy together,' Dilly said, pulling her into a hug. 'But remember, I want to use your business acumen for my fashion brand,' she said, releasing Eleanor long enough to point a finger in her direction. 'Together, we'll take the fashion world by storm!'

'Who's taking the world by storm?' Antony asked, returning from the bar.

'We are!' cried Dilly, her arms slinging across both Eleanor and Antony's backs, and she guided them onto the dance floor.

Barely an hour later and the crush of bodies was making Eleanor feel a little claustrophobic. Waving her hand at her damp neck wasn't even taking the edge off.

Antony was busy shouting, slightly drunkenly, into the ear of his best friend and Dilly was nowhere to be seen.

She tugged at Antony's jacket, but he waved her off. She just needed to get somewhere where she could breathe a little easier. Making her way towards the edge of the low domed hall where racks of wine bottles created little nooks, she ducked into one and welcomed the cooler air away from the press of bodies in the centre.

Her head fell back and she took a deep breath of much needed air. She'd not had a lot to drink, but more than she did usually and was hoping that she could avoid the nauseous way it made her feel sometimes.

She opened her eyes, startled to find herself almost toe to toe with Santo Sabatini. There he was, leaning insolently against the back wall, drink hanging lazily from the tips of long fingers, bow tie loose around his neck, looking more handsome than she cared to admit, glaring at her.

And, just like that, her moment of calm was snatched from her grasp. Instinctively, she leaned back, but too far and too quickly, and she was about to fall when his arm reached out and latched securely around her wrist.

Flames licked at her pulse point and connected to places around her body she'd not experienced before. He held her there, the taut lines of his arms connecting them as she read both surprise and confusion in his gaze, before he eventually tugged her forward to regain her balance and she felt foolish all over again. He removed his hand from her but she felt indelibly marked by his touch.

A derisive smirk pulled at a mouth she couldn't look

away from, even as she burned from the impact. His lips were different to Tony's. The bow of his upper lip curved in a subtle way, pressing sensually against the firmer, more angular shape of the one beneath it. Fascinated beyond rational thought, she took in the rest of his features, just like the year before. Having kept all thoughts of the powerful Italian carefully behind a locked door, her curiosity was let loose as her gaze raked over the hard angle of his jaw and across the firm lines of his mouth. Above those aquamarine eyes were dark brows, one of which was bisected near its end by a scar.

It made him seem so much *more* than Tony and his friends. Older, experienced...*knowing.*

That was what she saw in his eyes. *Knowing.*

'Had your fill, Princess?' he asked, not bothering to hide the humour he found in her fascination.

His derision was enough to cut through the heat that had begun to build deep within her, and straight to the heart of the shame she felt at finding anyone other than her fiancé remotely interesting.

She chose to ignore the taunt, for surely that was all it was. A cruel tease at her expense.

'You startled me, that's all.'

'I was here first, so that makes it *you* who startled *me*,' he said.

'You don't look startled. You look...angry,' she replied truthfully.

Something flashed in his eyes and the muscle at his jaw clenched reflexively. 'I get that a lot,' he said in a tone she couldn't quite decipher.

He raised his glass and took a mouthful of amber liquid without taking his gaze from her face. So why had she suddenly become incredibly conscious of herself? As if she thought he was trying to avoid looking at any other part of her.

'If you're expecting my congratulations, you'll be waiting some time,' he informed her in a bland tone.

The about-turn of their conversation pulled her focus back to Tony, or perhaps it wasn't an about-turn. Was he angry that she was engaged? She dismissed the thought as ludicrous.

But clearly whatever moment they had shared last year, whatever intimacy she had imagined might have formed between them, was gone. And in its place rose a defensiveness Eleanor wasn't used to.

'I suppose common decency would be too much to hope for,' she bit back.

'And there I was on my best behaviour,' he replied.

'Formality is not civility,' she reprimanded.

Something like surprise passed across his gaze before it was quickly masked, and somewhere deep inside her she preened at the realisation that she had caught him off-guard. Before his next words landed with all the weight of a prize punch.

'Civility?' he repeated with a laugh. 'You're marrying Antony Fairchild. The boy is rash and callow at best. Spoilt and mean at worst. You have only my commiserations,' he said with a wave of his glass.

'Are you drunk?' Eleanor demanded, shocked by his rudeness.

'Sadly, not enough,' he replied as if genuinely upset by the thought.

'Antony is not like that,' Eleanor said, ignoring his response.

And as if her words had sprung him to life, Santo closed the distance between them, peering down at her from nearly a foot of height above, and said, 'Illuminate me, Princess. Just how is it that your fiancé is none of those things?'

Her heart trembled in her ribcage, the scent of whisky, the woodsy trace of his aftershave, the heat of his body pressed close to hers, and everything in her felt...electrified. Something forbidden and dark shivered deliciously across her skin and made her squirm deep inside.

Santo looked at her again as if sensing the warring within her, as if knowing what was happening to her when she didn't even know herself. His gaze flickered between her eyes and her lips and for a heart-stopping moment she thought, *hoped*, that he might actually kiss her.

With a self-control he wasn't used to exercising, Santo stepped back from Eleanor and the moment. It would have been so easy. So easy to take what she didn't know she was offering, to give what she didn't know she needed. But to do so when she was so young, so innocent still, engaged or not...that would be unconscionable. He didn't play with girls who didn't know what they wanted, nor women who wanted more from him than he was willing to give.

He'd not been surprised by the news that she had become engaged, but the disappointment he'd felt was that it was Antony Fairchild of all people. He hadn't been lashing out at Eleanor when he'd called the Fairchild brat those things—Antony really was that and more. But Pietro had only asked that he make sure that Eleanor was safe, not to guard her from her own terrible choices. But was it really her choice, when Edward Carson would use Eleanor to make a financial match that would suit him and his business? Whether she knew it or not, if it hadn't been Fairchild it would have been someone else.

His chain of thought led him to the argument he'd had with his mother. One that still rang in his ears.

'Find a good girl, Santo... Settle down, Santo... Make me grandbabies, Santo...'

It amazed him that she couldn't understand why he had absolutely no intention of doing such a thing.

Eleanor looked at him, hurt still shimmering in her eyes from his callous words, and shame rose, strong enough to make him regret them.

'I apologise.'

She nodded in a way that told him he wasn't forgiven in the least.

'Truly,' he added sincerely, which seemed to soften her slightly.

He was in a foul mood. Between his mother and the demands of the Sabatini Group, he was having a rough year. The wildfires had come again and the Sabatini olive groves were suffering, along with a large section of Southern Italy and other parts of Europe. But no one seemed to want to invest in the kind of infrastructure that would actually tackle an immediate, on the ground response to the climate emergency that had near global reach.

He rubbed at his temple with the thumb of the hand that held the glass of nearly finished whisky and Eleanor seemed to look a little more closely at him this time.

'Are you okay?' she asked.

'Just a headache.'

'Yes, I've heard that whisky is the best cure for that,' Eleanor said tartly, and he couldn't help it. He threw his head back and laughed.

She might be an innocent, and impossibly young, but that made it all the more delightful when she surprised him with her wry sense of humour. The slight curve to her tightly pressed lips was a sucker punch he wasn't expecting though.

She rolled her eyes and looked away. And the moment she did, his gaze hungrily consumed her. The panels of the teal-coloured silk of her sleeveless dress clung to her body in a way that showed both her youth and her vitality as well as a promise of the woman to come. It was a heady combination for any man to see and she had no idea of the impact she made. None at all.

He pulled himself back from the brink of something monumentally stupid just as she returned her attention to him, castigating himself silently.

'Is it about the olive groves? Were they badly damaged by the fires?' Eleanor asked, wiping all trace of his immediate thoughts from his mind.

She knew about his business? He bit back his shock. All this time he'd been secretly keeping tabs on her it had not crossed his mind once that she might do the same to him.

'A little,' he admitted. 'But we'll survive.'

'We?' she asked, confused.

'Yes, me. My staff. *We*,' he clarified, and this time she seemed surprised. Knowing Carson, she'd probably only heard business discussed as to how it affected the singular, with no thought to the staff or the wider impact.

He watched her thoughts pass over her features, their expressiveness almost a wonder to see.

'Do you want some?' he asked, when he was able to regain his composure. 'I'll let you have some if you promise not to spill it over me,' he teased gently, knowing that he should never have asked.

She looked over her shoulder and back at the crowds.

Go, the angel on his shoulder urged. *While you still can.*

While I'll still let you, the devil whispered. A devil he ruthlessly pushed back to hell.

'Will you stop being such an arse if I do?' she asked, looking back at him.

'Probably not,' he replied, hiding the grin that tugged at his lips as he reached for the bottle on the floor beside him.

He stood up, surprised to hear a 'Yes,' come from where Eleanor had been standing.

'We'll have to share,' he said of the glass he waved between them. 'Still staying?'

She nodded, dropping her gaze, before closing the distance between them. For a moment he couldn't work out her intention, his pulse reacting to the sudden new proximity to her. Until she came to stand beside him against the brick wall.

'Wait—' He stopped her before she could lean back as he had been doing. Shrugging off his jacket, he slipped it around her shoulders. The dust on the wall would have ruined her dress, but it also would have given her hiding place away. He'd witnessed the telltale signs of one not-so-secret assignation already and he had absolutely no intention of letting unfounded rumours damage Eleanor's reputation.

She shrugged into it, the tuxedo jacket drowning her petite frame, and had to look away. Who would have thought the mere sight of her in an item of his clothing would make such an impact on him?

Bracing his body to ward off the unwanted arousal threatening to make itself known, he reached for the bottle of whisky and poured the sixteen-year-old Lagavulin Special Release into the glass before passing it to Eleanor.

'So, what are you hiding from?' he asked, genuinely curious.

'It just got a little hot out there in the press of people,' she said before taking a sip.

He wondered if that was all it had been, but had no intention of pressing further. His purpose here was to make sure she was safe, not monitor her for truths and falsehoods.

'What's your excuse?' she asked, passing him the glass back.

He took a mouthful and relished the peat on his tongue and the burn on his throat, the way the alcohol filled the cave of his mouth, and as he looked at Eleanor he noticed that her cheeks had flushed from her own mouthful.

'I was looking for some peace and quiet.'

'Well, you came to the wrong party,' she observed, as if uncomfortable with the noise and press of bodies out there in the larger area of the wine cellars.

'That I did,' he agreed, swirling the amber liquid around the glass in his hand.

There was a pause.

He opened his mouth to speak when a noise near the wine stacks stopped him.

'Here...in here.'

They both heard her fiancé's voice at the same time. Santo looked to Eleanor, whose eyes had widened in panic, presumably not wanting to be found in a dark corner with Santo. A mean part of him almost wanted it, wanted to see what that boy would do, but just when he expected that confrontation, he realised that no one was there.

He stepped forward just as a feminine giggle could be heard from over the wine stacks.

'Shh, you have to be quiet,' Tony could be heard saying.

'You told me you'd get away,' a whining voice replied.

'What did you want me to do? She hasn't left my side all evening.'

Santo turned to Eleanor just in time to see her realise what was going on, her eyes wide, skin pale, her lips opening to speak. He placed a firm hand over her mouth before she could. She wrestled against the arm he wrapped around her to stop her from rushing out to confront her cheating fiancé. She clearly couldn't see the situation she was in.

The entire group of families had talked of nothing else than their engagement from the moment it had happened. The joining of two dynasties had always been a long-held dream and, whether she knew it or not, Edward Carson wouldn't let go of it easily.

'Wait,' Santo whispered in her ear. 'Just wait.'

He looked her dead in the eye and waited until she registered his words, anger and confusion as easy to read as words on a page until she blinked them away and he saw sense return.

Her eyes narrowed and slowly she nodded.

'Oh, God, you don't know what you do to me,' the woman's voice moaned. 'I need you, Tony. *Now.*'

Santo didn't recognise the woman's voice, but from the sudden spark in Eleanor's eyes it was clear that she had. Tears began to gather in the corners of her eyes and it was the one thing, the only thing, that Santo had never been able to stomach.

'Stop,' he whispered harshly. 'Don't even think about shedding a tear over that bastard or whoever he is with. You *have* to be stronger than that.'

She blinked slowly, a tear escaping over her cheek. He swept it away with the pad of his thumb, but more tears seeped into the fingers still across her lips.

His gut clenched to see them. Anger, swift, sure and poker-hot, turned his gaze red. Helplessly, Eleanor looked up at him, begging him to take this away, to make it not be happening. And, just like that, he was back home with his mother and his father. And, just like then, there was nothing he could do to make it go away.

He closed his eyes, needing to take a moment, needing to push back the anger that combined a devastating past with the dangerous present. By the time he had regained control, Eleanor was looking at him with concern. He took his hand away from her mouth.

'Where is your phone?' he whispered.

'In my bag,' she said, offering up the small clutch that hung on a strap from her wrist. He grabbed it and pulled out the slim mobile.

'The PIN,' he demanded, showing her the screen.

With shaking fingers, she typed in the four-digit code that unlocked her phone. He found the app he wanted and turned on his heel.

Eleanor stood there shaking, unable to move. Unable to follow Santo around to the other side of the wine stack to where she knew what she would find.

Tony, her fiancé, and Dilly, her supposed best friend, having sex.

She couldn't believe it. She wanted to howl until she couldn't hear those noises any more. The betrayal coursing through her made her feel utterly wretched. How had she missed it? How had she been such a fool?

Too many thoughts, too many questions crowded her mind. If she'd slept with Tony, would this be happening? Was it her own fault? Had she somehow brought this on herself? Or had this been going on before their engagement? How could they do this?

The dizziness caused by all the questions made her

sway and she was beginning to slide to the ground when Santo came back around the corner. He reached for her and pulled her against him. And for just a moment she sank into him. Into his strength, into the protection he offered her, the strength of him.

He gave her that one moment before drawing her away from what Tony and Dilly were doing. She let herself be tugged along by the sheer power and determination of Santo, despite wanting to do nothing more than sink to the floor and cry.

'What did you do with my phone?' she asked with numb lips.

'Pictures.'

'You took pictures?' she demanded, outraged. 'Of *that*? Of *them*? Why would you—'

'Keep your voice down,' he all but growled, casting looks about them to see if she had drawn any attention to them.

When he had taken her as far away from her fiancé as he was apparently comfortable with, he pushed her gently back into another recess on the opposite side of the wine cellar.

Eleanor hastily wiped at the tears that had fallen on the way, scrubbing at her cheeks as she wanted to scrub at her eyes, her ears and her heart.

Oh, God.

'Listen, Eleanor—'

She started to shake her head. She didn't want to listen to anything. Tony had cheated on her.

'Eleanor,' he said, taking her shoulders and shaking her a little. 'You have to listen to me.'

Eleanor clenched her teeth together. 'Okay,' she said, even though all she could hear was Dilly's moans of pleasure, turning her stomach.

'They're going to tell you that it wasn't as bad as you think. They're going to tell you that it was just a mistake, that he loves you and that it's not worth throwing your future away for,' Santo said, his tone dark, his voice full of gravel.

Eleanor bit her lip, the tears building and acid scratching at the back of her throat, wanting to get out.

'Eleanor, are you listening to me?'

She wasn't, but she nodded, looking up to find Santo staring at her with an intensity that surprised her.

'Don't let them convince you it was nothing. If you feel yourself wavering, if you feel yourself thinking that they might be right, look at the photos. Don't let them force you into a marriage you don't want,' he commanded.

A low moan came from deep within her.

'Eleanor, this is important,' he said, shaking her by the shoulders a little.

'My father wouldn't do that,' Eleanor insisted, trying to pull out of his hold. 'When he finds out about this, he'll go mad. There's no way he'll let Tony get away with this.'

Santo looked back at her with pity in his eyes. As if she were being naïve. As if she didn't know her own father.

'He won't!' Eleanor cried out, pushing back against Santo. 'Why would you say that?' she demanded. 'Why would you even think that?'

Santo stilled, something dark filling his intent gaze. He opened his mouth to answer, but her mother's concerned voice came from over Santo's shoulder.

'Eleanor, are you okay?'

Eleanor pushed Santo aside and, shrugging off his jacket, she ran into her mother's arms.

With her head buried against her mother's chest and her eyes filled with tears, she didn't see the look that passed between Santo and her mother, Analise, and, even if she had, Eleanor wouldn't have cared. Her heart was breaking in two and she thought she'd never recover.

CHAPTER THREE

New Year's Eve seven years ago, Oxford

SANTO COULDN'T HELP HIMSELF. He didn't know whether
to be impressed or outraged by Edward Carson's ar-
rogance. Supposedly on the back foot after one of the
most shocking scandals ever seen by the group of twelve
families that met each New Year's Eve, the man was
hosting this year—at his own home—as if it were equal,
nay, even superior, to the exquisite locations of previous years.

It irritated Santo that this was, in fact, the case. It
might have been called Roughbridge House, but the
damn thing was a castle. It hadn't escaped Santo's notice that the greater the wealth, the greater the likelihood
that they would downplay it. As if calling a sprawling
Jacobean estate of nearly one hundred acres a 'house'
was a private joke amongst the higher echelons.

Guests were welcomed into the large entrance hall,
squarely positioned beneath more rows of mullioned
windows than Santo had ever seen before. Staff dressed
in black and white uniforms led those invited through
to various exquisitely decorated rooms with names like

'the salon' or 'the drawing room', quaint references to rooms with much less grandeur than the Carsons had on full display that evening. Santo scanned the faces of the guests, acknowledging and ignoring whoever he chose, but in truth he sought only one person.

Although Pietro had not expected him to keep tabs on Eleanor beyond these annual events, knowing that it would be too much of a risk to draw attention to himself in that way, it would have been nearly impossible to miss the headline news of the ending of her engagement. And once again Eleanor had surprised him, because seeing the way she'd run back to her mother last New Year's Eve, he'd thought she'd buckle, just like his mother had. But she hadn't. And while there had been much speculation on the reason behind the split, both camps were insistent that it was mutual and amicable.

Of course, behind the scenes it was a completely different story. The stock market changes read like a roadmap of retribution. Things had been quiet for the first few months, presumably while Eleanor was being convinced to maintain the engagement. And presumably, Eleanor proving immovable on the matter, Carson had gone on the offensive before the Fairchilds could do so. All of this was conjecture, of course. However, the jagged, angry slashes across shareholder prices and through the ownership signatures of both families' companies looked like a bloodbath. Rumour had it that the other families had been forced to intervene, bringing Edward and Archibald Fairchild to the table for peace talks.

Santo retrieved a glass of whisky from a passing waiter as he moved slowly from room to room. Antony's betrayal of Eleanor Carson had cost the Fairchilds billions. But what had it cost Eleanor?

She had interrupted his thoughts more than he liked over the course of the year. The way she'd looked up at him, so shocked and hurt.

'My father wouldn't do that.'

Santo shook his head. *Cristo*, he wondered what lessons she'd learned this year.

As he looked around the impeccably decorated ballroom, there was a heady sense of expectation amongst the gathering. It reminded him of some spectator event, as if it were the Colosseum, and the audience were waiting to be entertained. They were practically baying for blood.

He peered into the crowd, seeing the way that certain groups had gathered together. It seemed that in the aftermath of Eleanor's broken engagement, lines had been drawn and sides taken.

He caught sight of Antony Fairchild, his ruddy health only slightly dimmed by the events of the past year. Of Dilly Allencourt, Eleanor's so-called friend, there was no sign at all. Her father was here and her grandmother, but only those two. They had positioned themselves as far away from both the Carsons and the Fairchilds in the ballroom. He doubted they'd stay for more than an hour.

He was reluctantly impressed. Eleanor had singlehandedly achieved what no other person had done in the near five-hundred-year history of these gatherings; she had created divisions. And a ruthless person, a truly calculating one, could use that to their advantage.

If it had been any other year she might have got away

with not attending, but as it was Edward's turn to host it would be painfully obvious if she were absent. He thought of the girl he'd first met two years before and wondered if she had the strength to stand up to the scrutiny she was sure to be under. And for just a moment, he found himself wishing it could have been different for her.

'It's really quite something, don't you think?'

He turned to find Eleanor standing beside him on the fringe of the crowd.

'All these people, all this power. Money,' she clarified.

Santo nodded, something in his chest turning over at the realisation that she was finally beginning to see the truth about the people around her. And when he looked at her he could see the lines of maturity marked in her face. Slightly thinner cheeks, a knowing glint in her eyes, slightly harder than the sparkle that had been there in previous years.

'You survived,' he observed, relieved in a way he didn't want to examine.

Something passed quickly across her eyes. 'Just about,' Eleanor replied. A thin smile pulled at lips that deserved better. 'Can I borrow you for a moment?' she asked hesitantly.

He shouldn't, not really. There were too many eyes on her, but a connection had been formed between them. A connection that would only help him achieve the promise he'd made to Pietro. Severing it now could make it much harder for him in the future. And Santo would do nothing to jeopardise his vow to Pietro.

* * *

Santo nodded slowly and gestured for her to lead the way. Relief flooded through Eleanor, a strange and unfamiliar feeling these days, and she began to weave through the crowd towards the part of the house that was off-limits to the guests.

It had cost her more than she would ever admit to hold to what Santo had told her the year before. It had taken some of her innocence, a lot of her naivety and more strength than she'd thought herself capable of.

But finally, Santo was here. This was what she'd wanted, what she'd waited for. Through all the months following the awful argument that had broken out between her, Tony and her father, shortly after New Year. Through all the horrible predictions that Santo had made coming true, she'd clung to one single thought: that at least she'd see him again.

She wasn't quite sure how, but he had become the point on her map that was fixed, allowing her to find her North Star. She had told herself that if she could just get here, just see him again, that maybe things would be okay. Because somehow last year he had become her armour. Her protection. She'd reminded herself of his words and had clung to them with a ferocity that had surprised both Tony and her father. It had surprised even herself.

A familiar laugh resounded from the living room, casting a shiver across her skin. It was edged with cruelty— Tony, as if he were taking pleasure in the fact that he was here, in her home, despite all that had passed between them. The last time she had seen him had been horrible for her. The things that were said, the anger she had seen in him had shocked her terribly.

She had believed that this was someone she loved, someone she would spend the rest of her life with. It was unimaginable to her now. So much so that sometimes she wondered if she'd gone a little mad.

But she hadn't. Nor had she forgotten what Santo had said. Without that, Eleanor honestly thought that she might have actually taken him back. Tony and her father had persisted in their near constant attempts at persuasion for months, until Eleanor had sent the photographs to Tony's father, informing him that if he didn't take his son in hand, the images would appear on the front cover of several internationally respected newspapers.

The fallout had been devastating. Not because Tony's father had ignored her, because he hadn't. It was *her* father who had been the cause of her greatest hurt. She had never disappointed him before, and the sharp sting of it had been brutal. As if she'd lost the warmth of the sun from her life, the coldness harsh and visceral.

She turned back to the party to make sure they weren't spotted, before leading him up the back stairway to the library on the second floor. She could have laughed at herself, feeling as if she were sneaking around her own home. But these days she felt like a stranger here. Uncomfortable. Aware of everything. Trying not to put a toe out of line, when she wasn't the one who had done something wrong.

Behind her, Santo's presence felt solid, constant. He wasn't tiptoeing around, yet moving through the house as if it were more natural to him than her. His confidence...it was something she yearned for. Admired.

She reached the door to the library that had become her refuge in the last months. Her father was rarely home these days, and her mother let her have the space Eleanor had desperately needed. She hovered on the threshold, aware of how...*intimate* it felt to have Santo, a near perfect stranger who had changed her life so dramatically, in her personal space.

She opened the door and stood back to let Santo in, following him with her eyes as he walked to the middle of the room, lit solely by the gentle flames in the open fireplace. Shelves of books framed an old writing desk in front of a large bay window that, during the day, looked out over the manicured garden and the hedgerow maze. But now deep green, thick velvet curtains were closed against the wintry night. Santo scanned the photographs on the desk, one of her and her brother, one of her and her parents. The one of her and her father there to remind herself of the hope that things would return to the way they had been before.

'That's Freddie. My brother,' she said, coming to stand beside him, a smile on her lips as she looked at her little brother staring up at her with nothing but love. 'He's a terror. He's ten and thinks he knows everything.'

'I'm sure you have absolutely no idea what that feels like,' Santo observed wryly.

'He's the best thing in my life,' she replied with all the love she felt. 'Do you have siblings?' she asked, the smile on her lips dissolving as the air between them cooled, remembering too late the scant bits and pieces of his life she'd managed to find out online.

'No,' he said, the absence of inflection more damning and powerful than any emotional declaration could have been. And somehow she instinctively knew that whatever kind of relationship she had, or would have, with this man, it would never be one for small talk.

He took one glance back at the photographs, pausing on the one of her parents before turning to lean back against the table, his arms crossed as if impatiently waiting. He probably wanted to get back to the party. She should just say what she wanted to say and let him leave.

'I wanted to thank you,' she said, forcing herself to meet his gaze.

'For?' he asked, the Italian inflection in his clipped words harsher than she remembered.

'For what you did for me last year. I... My entire life would be vastly different if you hadn't said what you did.'

'You don't regret it?' he asked. She felt the impact of his observation, the touch of his gaze as soft as feathers, as if he were looking for signs of dishonesty.

'No,' she said, allowing him to read the truth in her face. 'But... I was ashamed that you were right,' she said, looking down at the floor. 'About everything.' She'd been so sure that he was wrong that night—the warnings he'd given her—but he hadn't been.

'I hated you for that at the beginning,' she admitted, thinking of those first few months when everything was still so raw. 'A part of me wanted it to just go away. To

pretend it hadn't happened. But I couldn't. Because of
the pictures.'

Santo's gaze never left her once, his expression un-
readable in the dim light cast by the fire.

She bit her lip. 'I didn't know my father could be like
that,' she confessed.

Her sigh shuddered out from her chest and Santo felt it
deep in his soul. It was a strange thing to hear because
Santo had always known. He'd grown up knowing, as if
it were instinctive—as if it were an awareness that he'd
opened his eyes to from the very beginning. It had made
it almost impossible for him to believe that she couldn't
see Edward Carson for what he truly was.

Yet in Eleanor he could still see the child that was
desperate for her father's love. Whether or not she could
instinctively sense that love was conditional, he could
hardly guess. But it wouldn't help her or him to burst
that bubble—it was something that could only be discovered for herself.

But something had eased in his chest to hear her
admit that she didn't regret her decision to end the engagement. A breath he hadn't realised he'd held almost
through the entire year released, replaced by satisfaction
that he had been right to do as he had done last year. Satisfaction that he had fulfilled something of his promise
to Pietro, even if it had come much sooner than either
of them had imagined. Santo didn't believe that his vow
was fulfilled though. Eleanor was still very much in-
fluenced by the people under this roof and, as such, not
entirely as safe as she believed. But it would do for now.

She was watching him closely and he was content to let her for the moment. What he had to hide from her was hidden too well for her to discern, and what he didn't, he was content for her to see. He nearly smiled at how easy it was for him to read her, seeing the expressions shifting across her pretty features—curiosity, hesitancy…something more that he didn't quite want to name. She would need to learn to hide her emotions much better.

'Spit it out,' he said, not unkindly, but he could feel delicate strands reaching out to bind them together and he couldn't afford it. And Eleanor, whether she knew it or not, most definitely couldn't afford it.

'How did you know?' she asked. 'How did you know that they would do what you said they would?'

If Santo was honest with himself, he'd known that she would ask it eventually. The scales had fallen from her eyes over this last year and he could tell she wasn't the naïve girl he'd first met two years before.

'Because that's what they told my mother,' he replied on an exhale, turning away from Eleanor and stalking towards the fire, the crackle and pop of the wood at odds with the pull of memories tugging him back to dark places. 'When she was having last-minute doubts, they lied to her and told her that he would change once he was married. When he *settled down*. They lied, Eleanor, because her marriage benefitted them financially. They do it time and time again. Anything to make money. Anything to keep that money.'

He turned to take in the room. The money in here was hidden well, but still there. The carpet beneath his feet, handmade silk from some far-flung corner of the world, bought by some unknown ancestor long ago. The desk, deep, rich wood and hand-carved. It would have been considered exquisite by many, but Santo couldn't help but see it as something that his father would have lusted after. Gallo Sabatini had wanted nothing more than the legitimacy of Eleanor's world. He'd hated his own family because *'they came from nothing and they died as nothing'*, his father used to snarl—often as a warning to him and his mother. As if he could one day make sure that they suffered the same fate, should he want to.

Gallo had bullied, blackmailed, stolen, beaten and eventually married his way into his empire and had never been able to sand down the rough edges of that dirt. And the greatest pleasure Santo had ever had was burying the man beside a family he'd resented for being backward, illiterate and miserable.

'You hate them?'

'Yes, I do,' he replied truthfully.

'Then why are you here? Why do you still come to these parties?'

Words halted on his tongue, struck silent by the desire to answer her and the promise he'd made to the man who had protected his mother when he, himself, had not been able to.

'She can never know, Santo. It would change her life irrevocably. It would put her in too vulnerable a position.'

But it wasn't just his vow to Pietro that kept him bound to this group of people, that kept him bound to Eleanor.

'Because while I gained an empire on his death, I am also shackled to it.'

She stared back at him, thoughts crossing her features like the turning of pages.

'What was he like, your father?'

'Violent, ugly and mean,' he replied, refusing to sugar-coat it for her when clearly so much of her life had been cushioned and softened.

'Is that where you got the scar?' she asked, her hand lifting almost to touch the mark that cut through his eyebrow.

He leaned away from her touch, the sudden shocking memory of how it had happened taking him by surprise when his defences were down. He clenched his teeth together until his jaw ached.

'Yes,' he said, turning away from her, not wanting to see her reaction.

The puff of exhaled air was barely audible over the crackle of the fire taking hold, but he heard it.

'I... I'm sorry.'

He huffed out a bitter laugh. 'What for? The man was a bastard—that's not your fault.'

Her silence filled the small room, pressing against him in ways he'd not experienced before. Finally, he looked up, only for the sympathy in her gaze to cut him off at the knees.

'Your father shouldn't have done such a thing.'

Her words turned over something in his chest that he didn't want to see. He never talked to anyone about his father. Not his mother, not even Pietro. And yet here

Eleanor was, smashing through all the barriers he tried to put around the subject.

'Fathers are just men, Eleanor, nothing more,' he said with a weight she wouldn't understand yet. 'Sometimes they make mistakes,' he said, thinking not of his own, but hers.

'Was that what your father did? Make a mistake?' she asked, taking a step forward.

'No. He knew what he was doing,' Santo said with an honesty that he'd never revealed to anyone other than Pietro.

Anger and tension swirled headily in his chest, reaching for the back of his neck in an aching hold. But Eleanor held his gaze and her nod to herself as much as him, her gentle acceptance of the violence that had shaped his life, rather than shock at it or refusal of it, calmed him in a way he'd not experienced before, in a way that shouldn't have been possible from the spoiled daughter of one of England's richest families.

All along she had been a contradiction. From managing to replace the shirt she'd spilled her drink on, so smoothly and seamlessly, to her ability to empathise so easily. Santo had written her off as a spoilt heiress, but she was steadily proving herself to be a puzzle. One he wanted to understand much more than he should.

'What will you do now?' he asked, moving the conversation onto the kind of small talk he usually loathed.

Eleanor smiled, recognising his diversionary tactic. But it was probably for the best. They had skated too close to topics that were intimate in a way she wasn't ready for. He made her feel things that were too familiar, yet utterly alien.

She knew enough to both recognise her attraction to him but to be wary of it too. It was probably some silly infatuation because he'd been there to rescue her when she'd needed it. And it was something she sensed he wouldn't welcome.

'I started my degree in September. I'll continue on with that,' she said, thinking of the arguments she'd had with her father, who had wanted her to stay here at the house, rather than move into the halls of residence at her university.

'What are you studying?'

'Business,' she replied, bracing herself against the derision he seemed to assume so quickly around her, but it never came.

'It's a good degree, with a lot of fundamentals that can be built on with experience. I found it useful.'

'You did a degree?' she asked, shocked.

His brow raised, eyes wry. 'That surprises you?'

'Yes,' she admitted. 'But only in so much as not knowing where you found the time for it.' She knew that he'd inherited the Sabatini Group upon his father's death, and that it had been held in trust for the sixteen months it took for him to reach eighteen. But she'd always assumed that he hadn't had time for something like a degree.

'I studied at night,' he admitted. 'But if you tell anyone, I'll deny it,' he vowed with mock seriousness.

His humour made her smile, but she recognised it as yet another diversionary tactic, keeping her at arm's

length. Despite that, she could still recognise the sheer
amount of work he must have done to not only maintain
his father's business but grow it, all the while complet-
ing a degree.

'Why did you do it?' she asked, unable to keep her
curiosity at bay. Every little piece of information made
her hungry for more.

His pause made her wonder if he was debating how
honestly to reply.

'I wanted something that couldn't be taken away from
me,' he said finally, the ring of truth in his words.

And there it was. The same desire she had. To have
something fully for herself. Something that she would
always have. After the shocking loss of the future she'd
thought she'd have with Tony, her degree had become
something that she'd clung to whenever she felt at sea.
It was a need for something solid, something *hers*.

'Did it work? Did it give you what you needed?' she
asked hopefully.

'Yes…and no,' he replied. Again, she appreciated
his honesty, even as she found his answer disappointing. She'd wanted reassurance, even if it were fake. The
promise that things would all be okay. But she would
never get that from Santo Sabatini and she didn't know
whether that was a good thing or a bad thing.

The flames in the fireplace were beginning to die
down. It would be time to go back to the party soon.
Eleanor knew she couldn't stay up here for ever. Certainly, she couldn't be caught up here with Santo. And
her father would send someone looking for her eventually. But she didn't want to leave just yet.

Santo was watching her, as if reading her thoughts in her expressions. It wasn't intrusive in the way that she felt from many of the other guests, especially this evening. But it made her feel…lacking in some way. As if he were looking for something that wasn't there in her yet.

She'd heard the rumours about him and Marie-Laure. The widow was beautiful, clever, sophisticated, powerful in a way that intrigued her, whilst also making her strangely jealous. It was a confidence, a self-belief that was so strong it was almost alienating. And Eleanor wondered whether she would ever be anything like the other woman.

'I'm keeping you from the party,' she said eventually, acknowledging the silence in the room.

'Yes,' he said simply.

She nearly huffed out a laugh, whether he'd meant it to be funny or not. She would always get the truth from him and she was thankful for that.

'Well, Mr Sabatini,' she said, returning to formality as if she could undo the intimacy of their exchange as easily, 'thank you again.'

He nodded simply, the firelight taking slow, unfurling licks across his cheekbones, casting shadows across his powerful jaw line, across the hair curling ever so slightly at the collar of his shirt and jacket.

She held out her hand and in a flash she remembered their first handshake, the awkward mistiming of it, the trace of his hand at her fingertips. There was none of that this time. He took her hand in his, again, his gaze searching for something in her that she couldn't help him find. His palm against hers was slightly rough but warm, his grip firm, but held just a second too long. Because in that time she yearned for something more. For something she didn't dare name. For in her wildest dreams she couldn't imagine this man wanting from her what she wanted from him.

'Happy New Year,' he said, taking his hand back and leaving the room without a backward glance.

'See you next...' The door closed on her words. 'Year,' she finished to herself.

Things would be different, she promised herself. People would have got over the gossip about her and Tony and would have found something else to talk about. Next year, she wouldn't be defined by anything other than herself, she promised herself, hoping that perhaps then Santo would see in her what he'd been looking for.

CHAPTER FOUR

New Year's Eve six years ago, Berlin

'AND THAT'S WHEN I took his entire company with an ace high,' Allencourt guffawed, as if swindling someone out of their company with the lowest hand of cards was something to be proud of.

Santo rolled his shoulders, trying to shake loose the tension that had taken up residence earlier that day.

'He never forgave you,' Aksel Rassmussen said, shaking his head.

'My conscience is clear,' Allencourt replied, and Santo nearly choked on his drink.

'More champagne, sir?' a waiter asked.

Santo shook his head. 'But I'll give you fifty euros for a glass of whisky.'

'It's a free bar,' whispered the waiter, leaning in.

'I know,' Santo whispered back drily, the poor kid not knowing what to say. Santo laughed, more at himself than the waiter, and waved the boy off.

There was something about humour that no amount of language lessons could teach. And that, he realised, was just another thing that set him apart from the people here. Or most of the people here, he thought as he caught sight of Mads making his way across the sprawling nave in the most beautiful church in Berlin's Kreuzberg district.

Santo felt rather dubious about celebrating the annual New Year's Eve event in a church. He might not have been particularly religious himself, but it still skated close to the line that apparently didn't worry the Müllers.

Gunter Pichler passed close by, glaring at him. Santo blanked the man completely, trying to keep the victorious smile he felt from escaping onto his features. Just that morning he'd received yet another begging email from Pichler, wanting to resume his investment in the Sabatini Group. Surprisingly, Santo had had a good year, better than some had expected—some, like the Pichlers, had chosen to cash in their shares and now bitterly regretted it. His lips curled into a bitter smile. *Good riddance.*

Unconsciously, he scanned the crowd, not quite sure what he was looking for. No matter the jewels displayed by the guests, it was the church's magnificence that truly shone. The high domed ceilings were nothing short of an architectural feat, even though the gentle neon blue and purple lighting felt out of place and strangely inappropriate.

The drawn lines from last year were nowhere in sight. He spotted Carson laughing with Dilly's grandfather, and Analise Carson talking to Archibold Fairchild. No matter how well Eleanor was doing, she couldn't have been happy with such a painfully obvious 'business as usual' message being conveyed by the families.

And he ruefully wondered what 'business as usual' would look like for his family, and bitterly regretted the harsh words he'd exchanged with his mother last week. Santo had discovered that she had been visiting his father's grave in Puglia, maintaining it and keeping it clean. It had been their worst argument yet. There was simply too much between them to be able to speak clearly on it. Too much hurt, too much guilt.

But their raised voices had skated too close to the past. His mother's fearful retreat from him was too much to bear. Santo gritted his teeth against the wave of hot, sickly emotion that always came when he thought of such things. Guilt, hatred, fear.

He was distracted from his thoughts by the gentle probe of someone's gaze. Curious, he looked deeper into the crowd, searching for someone his mind hadn't quite caught up to. Because he recognised that feeling. The warmth, the heat that he tried to ignore. The spark that shouldn't be there.

But he couldn't ignore it because there she was.

Eleanor.

From across the room, she flashed him that little Mona Lisa smile that might just be for him alone, the thought touching him much deeper and stronger than he realised. She inclined her head, and he did the same in acknowledgement, and her smile kicked up just a little more.

She gave a slight frown, her gaze flickering between him and the company he was in—as if she were surprised—and he couldn't help but roll his eyes, their silent conversation communicating his boredom and frustration with the men bragging about destroying each other's businesses.

Whoever she was talking to called back her attention. Glimpses of her kaleidoscoped across his vision as other guests passed back and forth in between them, reminding him of the bits and pieces of information he'd picked up about her throughout the year.

She had proved a little more distracting this year, his curiosity such that he'd had to find a particularly unscrupulous individual working at the university offices where Eleanor studied to keep him updated on her progress, so as not to derail his working day. He'd been pleased, and not as surprised as he once might have been, to discover that she was excelling in her courses. The unique twist of something like pride overrode any concerns his conscience might have had—he was simply keeping his word to Pietro.

He was about to take a sip of his drink when the man obscuring his view of her moved and he was able to see her fully for the first time. His hand hovered in the air, paused, in the time it took to take her in. And while everything in him roared against the inappropriateness of noticing what he most definitely should *not* be noticing, he couldn't help himself.

She was beautiful.

He'd always known that, in some distant part of his mind. In fact, if he was honest with himself, it was what had driven him from her company last year. An awareness of her that felt so wrong next to an innocence that practically screamed in warning.

But he had overestimated his confidence in her youth

as a barrier to his increasing interest, as the person talking to the red-haired daughter of Artur Kivi was clearly
no longer an innocent adolescent. And so it was that,
with a shock of realisation, Santo now recognised Eleanor as a young woman of twenty-one, only five years
his junior.

Her hair, artfully piled on top of her head in a messy
bun, showed off the swanlike curve of her neck. The
thick velvet sleeveless dress moulded to her torso and
veed across her chest in straps that tied on top of her
shoulders, leaving her toned arms and sternum completely bare. Skirts dropped in dramatic folds from her
waist to hit her mid-calf, the shape of her legs turning
into delicate ankles topped with indecently high heels.

Never before had anyone taken such a swift hold of
his body and Eleanor Carson had done it effortlessly
and unconsciously in the space of a heartbeat. Santo
was about to turn away before he made a fool of himself in public, when she caught his eye once again and
this time her smile was unrestrained.

And the slash of lightning that struck him stole his
breath.

Eleanor tried to cover the word she'd stuttered over
the moment she'd caught Santo Sabatini staring at her,
and failed miserably. Because this time they weren't
exchanging subtle, easy interactions across a crowded
room. No, this time, she'd felt heat. Interest. Want. The
very things that severed her thought processes enough
for her to forget her words.

'I'm sorry, Kat, I completely forgot where I was for a moment,' she admitted helplessly.

Ekaterina smiled. 'That's okay. We were talking about Capri.'

'Oh, yes,' Eleanor remembered vaguely, and shook her head, trying to dislodge the impact Santo had made. 'How did you find it?' she asked. But, no matter how hard Eleanor tried, she couldn't quite focus on Kat's answer.

She flicked her gaze to where Santo had been, but he was no longer there. Which was strange, because she could still feel the weight of his attention on her. She rolled her shoulders, enjoying the way that the thick black satin-lined velvet pressed against her skin.

Her father had barely spared her a glance, but Eleanor had loved the dress the moment she'd seen it. It made her feel like a *woman*. And she'd so desperately wanted to feel that way tonight. Not a naïve, foolish girl who'd become engaged too soon, or a silly young miss stumbling over thanks as she had been last year. She'd wanted to be someone who could command attention. Command *his* attention.

But the moment she'd felt it, it had almost completely overpowered her. That full force impact had stolen her breath and her chain of thought, so much so that she could still feel the ripples of it now in the goosebumps across her skin.

'Oh, here he comes,' Ekaterina squealed. 'Please don't say anything,' she followed in a whisper.

Ekaterina's crush on Mads Rassmussen had been all her friend could talk about all evening, and Eleanor felt only a moment's jealousy. She knew that feeling, that sense of thrill as if glitter fizzed in one's veins and invisible fingers traced down one's spine.

Because it was how she felt about Santo—not that she'd ever dare say. There was something about their interactions that was private. Secret. And she wanted to keep it that way, especially after the painfully public fallout from her broken engagement.

Eleanor smiled at Mads as he joined them, but was distracted once again by the feeling of someone watching her. She told herself she was being fanciful, but she *knew* it was Santo. She knew it in a way that felt...*fated*.

'Don't you think so, Elle?'

Kat looked at her expectantly, and Eleanor nodded quickly.

'Absolutely,' she hedged, hoping it was the right thing to say, breathing out a sigh of relief when Kat smiled.

Mads looked at them both in mock horror. 'No, not me. I'd never do something like that,' he affirmed, and Kat playfully slapped him on the arm with a little too much strength.

Eleanor bit the inside of her cheek to stop herself from laughing. Kat would never be as subtle as she thought she was being, but it felt nice. Nice to be talking about unimportant things and enjoying someone else's happiness after the last two years' tumult.

'Ah, there you are, Santo, stop skulking and come and join us,' Mads called over Eleanor's shoulder.

Her breath caught and the ripples across her skin turned to shivers.

Santo came to stand beside her and she smiled and

looked away, not quite prepared for the stark impact of him yet. There was a sense that they were both battling to maintain a distance that had already been thoroughly destroyed, but it was almost part of the unconscious game they seemed to be playing.

'Have you two met?' Ekaterina asked, blissfully ignorant of the currents passing back and forth between them.

Eleanor panicked. What was she supposed to say? Nerves made words dry in her throat.

'Once, I believe,' Santo said for her.

'Yes,' she said, finally turning to him with a smile. 'It's nice to see you again.'

Santo tipped his head in acknowledgement, but the glint in his eye—the one just for her—teased and taunted in a way that thrilled her.

'Likewise,' he said.

Oh, God, he looked incredible.

All year she'd been thinking about him. Her starved imagination had forced her to search him online, although 'search' was a polite term for what many others would call stalking. But the sheer impact of his presence was something else entirely. She almost didn't know where to look first.

Dark hair, lazily curling, was shorter this year than it had been. The hollows of his cheeks were ever so slightly more pronounced, made so by a close-cropped beard punctuated by the slight cleft in his chin. But there was something in his eyes—so light they were nearly aquamarine—that meant she could hardly bear to hold his gaze. It was as if they refracted all that she was feeling and threw it back at her in glittering fragments, making her unsure what he felt or thought at all.

'Oh, I love this song,' Ekaterina cried, and Eleanor looked down at the ground with a smile of affection at the transparency of her friend's motives.

Santo glanced between Mads and Kat and raised an eyebrow.

'Would you...?' Mads started to ask.

'Oh, yes—yes, please. Let's dance,' Kat said, before practically dragging the poor man off to where a few of the others had begun to dance.

Eleanor looked back to Santo's carefully blank expression and smiled.

'What?' he asked, without looking her way.

Eleanor bit back her smile, enjoying her observation of him. 'I don't think you're as indifferent as you pretend to be.'

'I assure you I am,' he insisted as if offended, and this time she couldn't help it. She let the smile break out because their interactions made her feel as if she saw something that few people did. As if he gave her something of himself that no one else saw.

A waiter paused beside her and she took a glass, turning to Santo to make a toast.

'To the New Year,' she said.

'To the New Year,' he repeated, the clink punctuating their toast before they each took a sip.

'I hear congratulations are in order,' Eleanor offered.

'For me?' he asked as if surprised.

She huffed out a gentle laugh. 'Yes, for you. The Sabatini Group's turnover was nothing short of miraculous this year. And I heard you managed to rid yourself of one of your investors. That is no mean feat,' she added conspiratorially.

He frowned at her as if confused by her knowledge of his business. She frowned back exaggeratedly, receiving a begrudging smile in response—just as she'd hoped.

'Business degree, remember?' she reminded him.

'I do,' he confirmed, and those words meant more to her than he would ever imagine. It was like a present she'd been hoping for all year long.

Eleanor took a deep breath. It continued to be a bone of contention between her and her father. It was as if everything she did to please him took her further and further away from what she had meant to him before. Before she'd broken her engagement, before she'd ever started to attend these things.

Instinctively, she sought out her father in the crowd and noticed that he was looking their way. And suddenly she didn't want to be caught by her father with Santo, she didn't want to be out here where people could see them. She noticed more and more people looking their way.

'What's wrong?' Santo asked, feeling the change in her demeanour like a cloud passing over the sun. The smile that pulled up the corners of her lips became tighter.

'People are staring.'

She was right, of course. For himself, Santo had got quite used to the feeling, but it clearly upset her.

'Want to see something spectacular?' Santo whispered in her ear. She looked up at him, the gratitude in her eyes louder than a cry as she nodded, taking what he was offering with both hands.

Santo drew Eleanor away from the crowds and up the staircase at the back of the nave to a second floor. A narrow walkway took them beyond the pews that looked down onto the altar, to behind the focal point of the church.

He was aware of her with every step he took. It was madness to be alone with her, especially as he wrestled with the effect she was having on him, but the unwanted attention she was receiving had taken away that sense of confidence that had lit Eleanor from deep within and that was unacceptable.

He held his hand out to her as he guided her up the last few steps towards his destination. And when she placed her hand in his he tried to ignore the sparks that fizzled and hissed between their touch.

If he'd expected Eleanor to ask where they were going, he'd been mistaken. She appeared utterly at ease with wherever he was taking her. Perhaps she hadn't learned enough from the past few years then. She should be on her guard. Especially around him.

He headed for the large ornately designed window with slashes of stained glass segmented by thick dark metal bleeding into the night, making it appear almost magical. Next to the series of crossing steps, the entire area reminded him of an Escher painting, making him wonder how different things could have been for him. For her. For *them*.

Just as they reached the window a firework scattering yellow and pink bursts into the night sky exploded and

Santo heard a soft gasp of surprise fall from Eleanor's lips. And with just that Santo battled with a surprisingly fierce wave of arousal that shivered through his body.

He barely dared look at her. Up close, he could see that Eleanor's dress was made of a thick black velvet, studded with absolutely minuscule studs of gold that made it look as if she shimmered like the night sky on the other side of the window. The paleness of her skin, rather than seeming diminished, glowed within the material. And he was struck that the regality that she wore like a cloak across her shoulders had turned a princess into a queen. Something that made her feel so very far beyond his reach.

Another firework exploded and he watched the flares glitter in her eyes, the slight flush of pleasure on her cheeks, and indignation that he hadn't put it there himself was enough of a warning for him to step back. Only he couldn't seem to bring himself to do it.

But he really should. He was there to protect her, for Pietro, and that most certainly included protecting her from himself. The things he'd seen, the things he knew... they were too much for an innocent like Eleanor.

She closed her eyes and lost the sparkle of the night, as if somehow intuiting his attempt to withdraw from her.

'Your mother isn't here?' Eleanor observed without looking at him.

He was surprised, the turn in conversation yanking him out of his thoughts, and forced himself to answer the question. He supposed it was understandable, though.

For a gathering supposedly of families, his was notice-
ably absent, even considering Gallo's death.

'*I* represent the family,' he stated grimly, finding it
uncomfortable that perhaps he couldn't read her thoughts
as much as he'd believed.

'Does she not like all this?'

'No. She never did,' he said, wishing that they had
more than these silly glasses of champagne. He took
a mouthful of the bubbly alcohol anyway, the taste
of nothing but regret on his tongue. He looked down,
knowing that he could change the topic of conversation.
Knowing that she would accept it if he did, but for the
first time he found himself wanting her to know. About
him. About his childhood.

'She was an only child and her father was old when
she was born. He was desperate to marry her off, and
my father was desperate enough to take her name.'

Santo thought about how cruelly his mother had been
used by the men in her life, how awful it must have been
not to have anyone on her side. He wondered if that was
why he was drawn to Eleanor, to the similarities between them as much as the differences.

'I didn't realise. I thought your connection here was
through your father,' Eleanor said.

'He was happy to make it seem like that, and after
the money he made for many of the families here they
were happy to go along with it.'

He looked at Eleanor, staring up at him with those
wide eyes. He could see her hovering on the edge of innocence. Yes, she'd had her fingers burnt by Tony, by
Edward Carson's response to her broken engagement,

but it was just the tip of an iceberg he wasn't sure that she would ever be ready to face.

'I'm sorry. This is a heavy conversation to have when everyone around us is celebrating,' Eleanor said, recognising that Santo was close to shutting down, when all she wanted to do was open him up. She'd thought so much of him over the last twelve months, but knew almost nothing about him—other than what was mentioned in the business pages. But perhaps there was a different way, a *lighter* way?

'Would you like to play a game?' she asked, forcing a playfulness into her tone.

For a moment, she wondered whether he'd take her up on her offer.

'That depends on the game,' he said, something glinting in his eyes that pulled at her body.

'Truth or dare,' she replied.

He frowned, those dark brows closing down over the incredible aquamarine of his gaze.

'Have you not played truth or dare before?' she asked with a laugh.

'I have heard of it, but never played it.'

Reading between the lines, his childhood sounded dark, hard and painful, and she suddenly wondered just how much Santo had been able to play as a young boy. She was about to retract the offer when he asked, 'Who goes first?'

'I will,' she said before he could change his mind. 'Truth or dare?'

He huffed out a cautious laugh. 'Do I not get to know the question first?'

She shook her head slowly, a smile curving her lips.

He nodded once, and seemed to lean closer in, their bodies speaking their own language to each other.

'Truth,' he said then.

'Okay, but it's a hard one, so think carefully,' she warned. 'What is...your favourite food?'

Santo barked out a laugh and it warmed her then. She'd seen him cynical, bitter, hard, disdainful, but this was something she only occasionally saw when it was just the two of them alone and that made her feel... thrilled. Excited. As if perhaps there could be something here between them. Something more than just a passing fancy.

'It is a cliché but tiramisu. I could eat a whole bowlful every day,' he admitted, leaning against the wall beside the large, beautiful round window. 'Your turn,' he announced.

'Truth,' she said, answering his unspoken question.

His inhale and narrowed eyes were playful, but still she found herself unaccountably nervous, until his gaze raked her body from top to toe, making her feel something else entirely.

'Where are you ticklish?' he demanded.

She blinked. 'What makes you think I'm ticklish?'

'You're avoiding the answer,' he teased.

Eleanor huffed, trying hard not to let a smile escape onto her lips. 'My feet,' she replied mock resentfully.

He nodded to himself as if he'd thought as much.

'Truth or dare,' she challenged.

PIPPA ROSCOE   73

'Truth.'

'Who was your first kiss?' she asked, pressing her lips together the moment the words were out of her mouth, the fizzle and crackle no longer outside in the night sky but hurtling through her veins beneath her skin.

A gleam of surprise flashed in his gaze just as another round of fireworks exploded over the Brandenburg Gate.

'Sofia Barone,' he replied with a slow smile as if remembering. 'We were fourteen years old, and were supposed to be playing hide and seek with her brother. He didn't find us,' he replied, clearly proud of his achievement.

She doubted he knew it, but his entire expression had changed. His face had relaxed, for once losing some of the intensity that marked him as different to almost everyone else here. And it was as if the shadows that haunted his gaze had lifted for a moment. Before he shook his head, his eyes clearing from the memory and focusing on her.

She could see it. The temptation to ask her the same question, the debate, the war in him.

'Truth or dare?' he asked slowly.

'Truth.'

She wanted him to ask her about her first kiss. She wanted him to open the door, even just a little, to where she wanted to go. To what she wanted to do. The sensual pull she'd denied the year before had become insistent as she skated the edges of whatever this was between them. She wanted it to be something more. She needed it to be tangible.

'Did you sleep with Fairchild?'

Instantly her cheeks flushed. The raw gravel tone of his voice scratched over every sensitive part of her body. She should have been surprised by the question, but she wasn't. It had been there, simmering between them. She'd wanted it, Santo just had the confidence to dig that deep. Her heart thundered in one powerful pump, rushing blood through her body and making her skin tingle so much that she felt the echoes of it reverberating around her heart while she held her breath. She bit her lip, knowing that this was a line she couldn't come back from. That the door she had opened a little was about to be pushed further.

'No,' she said, holding his intent gaze. She wanted him to see the truth. To know it. 'Truth or dare?' she asked before she could chicken out.

'Dare,' he replied, sending sparks down into her core.

She closed the step between them, her heart in her throat, her pulse beating at a furious rate.

'I dare you to kiss—'

'Eleanor?'

Shocked, Eleanor spun round to come face to face with her father.

Edward Carson glared between her and Santo, and she took a step back just as Santo took a step forward, drawing her father's attention. Whether consciously or unconsciously, he had put himself between her and her father.

'Sabatini.'

'Carson,' Santo replied likewise.

Eleanor could feel the hostility between the two men, which seemed excessive for the context of the situation.

She had never asked whether her father had investments in the Sabatini Group, or whether Santo had investments in her father's businesses, but it was clear, whatever the case was, there was contention between the two.

'Come. We're leaving,' Edward announced, not even holding out his hand for her as he might once have done.

'I—'

'Do not try me, Eleanor,' her father warned.

Everything that had just been within her reach was slipping through her fingers like sand. She bowed her head, giving up the fight, and followed in her father's footsteps. Just before the last step took her away from Santo she looked up to find something like regret in his gaze, before it was quickly blinked away.

It gave her hope. It made her think that perhaps next year things might be different.

And Eleanor was right. Things *would* be different next year, but not in a way that she'd ever imagine.

CHAPTER FIVE

New Year's Eve five years ago, Paris

'OF COURSE THE Dubois wouldn't be so crass as to arrange their event at the Eiffel. It's been done to *death*.'

'Naturally. But this is...*acceptable*.'

'Quite,' came the insincere response.

Santo ground his teeth together and checked his watch. He was late and impatient. His eagerness to see Eleanor had grown into almost monstrous proportions now that he was actually here. The two elderly ladies, a Müller and an Allencourt, conversing in English, hovered by the entrance, in the way. One of them peered meanly over her shoulder at him, disdain evident the moment she recognised him.

Those of her generation had been less inclined to accept his father's marriage to his mother and, as such, less inclined to accept *him*. However, as he made them and their children obscene amounts of money they tended to consider him a necessary evil.

He flashed his most charming smile, with just enough wickedness to melt the ice in her gaze, before her friend pulled her through the entrance to the Pavillon Dauphine. The grand building, situated at the bottom of the Avenue de l'Impératrice, was over a century old and every inch of its grandeur was marked in classic lines of beauty throughout. But at that moment Santo Sabatini couldn't have given a damn for any of it.

He had one goal and intended to find her as fast as humanly possible. For almost the entire year he'd thought of little else. She had occupied his waking thoughts and tormented his sleep. The innocence of her request, the clear intention behind it, had driven him near wild with want. He'd almost begun to regret keeping tabs on her university career, the updates keeping him tied to her in a way he both wanted and loathed.

But then, a few months ago, something had changed. Her online presence had dropped away to nothing, with no mention of her or—more surprisingly—Edward Carson or his business. For a man who craved attention it was a little unusual. Then, a month ago, Santo had discovered that she had stopped attending class, making both him and Pietro deeply concerned. But no amount of digging had uncovered anything.

Santo stalked through the grand entrance and into the large sprawling conservatory, where a long dining table was overburdened with a spectacular feast, but the smell of the rich food only turned his stomach. Scanning the faces of those seated, he knew she wasn't there. He couldn't feel her presence.

He reached the lavish ballroom, one wall covered in large mirrors encased in ornate mouldings, honey-coloured wooden floors gleaming beneath the gentle lighting, and still there was no sign of her. Ignoring the way that the pace of his pulse had picked up in concern, he swept into the next room and the next, until he'd covered all the rooms bar the ladies' toilets.

Then, through the window, he saw that there were people gathered outside, beneath the warm glow of heaters. An outside bar had been set up, and smaller seating areas attracted the few that were braving the cold in their furs and finery.

Ignoring his usual distaste for such things, he approached the patio doors that would have taken him out onto the area gently illuminated by strings of fairy lights, searching for a single face from amongst the crowd.

Already he felt a twisting deep in his gut. The only people outside were from Fairchild's group. And with a blinding sense of betrayal, he knew she was there amongst them.

He hung back in a darkened corner of the room until he spotted her, laughing at something someone had said in a gauche way he had never before associated with her. The rage that he felt in that moment, the pure fury that she had gone back to the very people who would have used her, who had abused her, was a red haze that he could barely breathe through. His heartbeat pounded in his ears like a war drum and it took nearly everything in him to wrestle himself under control.

The realisation drained the blood from his head so quickly he became lightheaded. Because in that moment he'd felt a violence he'd only ever witnessed in his father. Instinctively and unconsciously, his hand went to his eyebrow, fingers pressed against the scar as a cold sweat lay in a fine sheen across his skin beneath the shirt and tuxedo he wore tonight.

He braced his palm against the wall, holding himself back, holding him *up*, knuckles gleaming white under the force of it.

How could she?

Past hurts mixed nauseatingly with the present as he almost violently forced himself back in line.

What had happened to him?

Behaving like some jealous schoolboy with his first crush. As if she had ever been anything more to him than a promise he'd made to an old man to whom he owed a debt.

In his mind, he wrote over the memories of their interactions, editing out the impact and the intimacy as if he could undo every effect Eleanor Carson had ever had on him. As if he could backpedal his feelings and shove them far back behind a line he had never crossed, and would never again.

He was done. He would fulfil his promise and no more.

Every single part of Eleanor was in agony. Her body, her soul, all buckling under the weight of the trauma that had taken everything she'd thought she knew about herself and those in her life and slashed a line through it all.

She laughed at something Ekaterina had said and it sounded as hollow and false as she felt. Resentment seethed beneath the surface as she reached for a glass of something she barely even tasted as she downed the alcohol, the faint buzz touching her senses but still not enough to take away the pain that cut at her lungs every time she took a breath.

She shivered, even though the heat from the outside lamps was such that many around her were without shawls or coats.

Tony slid a glance her way. Suspicion and anger mixed with that sense of snide superiority he could no longer hide from her. Because something had happened since she'd discovered the truth back in November, since her family had become something alien and unknowable to her. It was as if she could see through it all. The lies, the secrets, the bullshit.

She laughed to herself this time, uncaring of the concern in Ekaterina's face. For all Eleanor knew, that was as fake as the rest of them. She'd seen Dilly earlier in the evening, her one-time best friend giving her a wide berth. And suddenly the tears she'd been holding at bay pressed terrifyingly close to the corners of her eyes.

She bit her lip, hoping that the sharp sting would work to pull her out of that moment. The moment when she'd thought of how much she wished there was someone to confide in. Someone to seek help from. Support. *Love.* But all of that was gone.

She was on her own now in a way that had truly shocked her to her core. Because eight months ago she'd discovered that Edward Carson was not her father. And overnight he had become a complete stranger to her.

'Who is my father?' she'd cried, begged, pleading with her mother, whose own shock had been worn clearly on her ghostly white features, contrasting with the fierce red fury of her father's.

Eleanor looked around hazily at the sea of faces, wondering who—if anyone—knew. Or whether they could somehow tell that she wasn't Edward Carson's daughter. Were they all laughing at her behind her back? Had they always been?

No one can know. No one can ever know.

Little Freddie's blood drive to help the friend from school who'd been diagnosed with leukaemia had irrevocably changed the trajectory of her life. He'd happily gathered their donor cards together, ticking off each one of their blood types, blissfully unaware of the sudden, devastating change in room temperature. That evening, Freddie had been sent to his room without explanation and little drama because somehow, without explanation, he'd realised that something was terribly wrong.

The single slap across her mother's face delivered cruelly by the man she'd thought of as her father had broken something deep within her. But no matter how many times he'd asked, yelled or shouted, demeaned or bullied, her mother had refused to name her father. She had simply said, *'I don't know,'* over and over again, in the hope that either her daughter or husband might eventually believe her.

And then Edward Carson had turned on her.

'You listen to me, and you listen good. If you want to have even the smallest chance of maintaining any kind of relationship with your brother, not a word of this gets out. Ever,' he'd warned darkly. *'You'll go back to your friends, you might even find another fiancé. I don't care. All that matters is that none of this gets out.'*

As the words ran through her mind like a film reel, she knew that the worst was yet to come.

'I will not have it known that I let a bastard into my family and treated her like my own.'

A waiter passed with another tray of drinks and she took the glass of whisky, swallowing the tears that had gathered in her throat along with the peaty alcohol.

Everything felt wrong. Her skin crawled as if some dark nightmare had slipped over her and she couldn't escape it.

The man she had thought was her father, the man she had loved, the man for whom she had worked hard to become someone he could be proud of, had turned into a vicious monster. He had all but cast out her mother, allowing her to remain in the house only to save face.

And her brother—poor little Freddie who, having turned twelve over the summer, knew that something was wrong—had begun to retreat into himself, as if pole-axed by the secrets in the family. Yes, Eleanor could leave. But she didn't doubt for one minute that her father would prevent her from returning or seeing her brother while he remained under his roof. And what would happen to Freddie without her mother or her around to protect him?

She didn't think her father would do anything to him, other than mould his young, barely formed personality into whatever he wanted. And that, she was beginning to realise, was the most terrifying thing about the whole situation.

That her brother would lose his innocence. That he would be twisted and warped into her father's image.

That Freddie would become like these young men in the garden, laughing at whatever cruelty had taken their fancy.

Because that was what they did. They found something or someone and made them the butt of their jokes, casting them as an outsider to torment for their own amusement. And she didn't want Freddie anywhere near these people. Fighting back the cramp fisting her stomach, she threw back another mouthful of whisky, a drink she'd acquired a taste for two years earlier, with Santo.

Santo.

She knew he'd be here this evening. She thought that perhaps he might have come here with expectations. Expectations that she'd encouraged last year, back when she'd thought she'd survived the worst that life could throw at her.

A bubble of almost hysterical cynicism rose from deep within her.

Naïve. Foolish.

She knew that Santo had believed her to be both of those things. And he'd been right. All along, she had been incomparably naïve and utterly foolish. And now it seemed as if broken shards of rose-coloured glass lay at her bare feet, ready to cut her if she moved even an inch.

'Eleanor, are you sure you're okay?' Ekaterina asked, and she was about to reply when she felt it. When she felt *him*.

She swallowed, capable only of nodding her reassurance. Because if she opened her lips the only thing that would emerge was a miserable sob.

The hairs stood up at the back of her neck, goosebumps shivering over her skin. The weight of his attention was an icy finger trail across her shoulder blades, poking and prodding an accusation of betrayal and disappointment.

She could only imagine his shock at seeing her back here amongst the very people who epitomised everything he seemed to hate about this event. The very people she had turned her back on three years before. The very people that her father had blackmailed her into joining again.

'If anyone finds out, you'll never see Frederick ever again.'

And Santo would. He would find out, he would cut to the heart of her secret so effortlessly, and she couldn't allow him to do that. She couldn't risk it. So, with that threat ringing in her ears, she turned her back to where she felt Santo's presence and said to Ekaterina, 'Let's dance.'

'And that's when I told him that he could invest whatever he wanted, but that I was having nothing to do with it.'

'Quite right. So have you considered...'

Santo tuned out from the banal conversation of the men and women around him. It was always the same: who had the most money, where could that money be put to use, what could they get? This constant grab, grab, grab.

His gaze scanned the room, refusing to settle on Eleanor, but always keeping her within his line of sight. He clenched his jaw as, from the corner of his eye, he saw her wobble awkwardly on her heels. He hadn't been counting, but he could tell that she had already had more to drink that evening than all of the previous New Year's Eve parties put together.

Something was wrong.

And she hadn't come to him.

Old insecurities rose to the surface. Memories of being unable to do anything to protect his mother, of being helpless against his father. And then, just when he'd got big enough to fight back, his father had used her against him. The threat against her was the only leash that Gallo Sabatini had needed against Santo, and he'd used it well.

Until that last day. He'd heard the argument from outside the house. The screams that had caused the blood to freeze in his veins. Santo had rushed through the doors of the villa just outside Rome and found his mother crouched over his father's broken body lying at the bottom of the curved staircase.

With shaking hands, she'd pulled her mobile from her pocket. He'd honestly thought she'd been calling the police until he'd heard her begging Pietro to come. When his mother had looked up and found him standing there...

He'd never forget the look on her face.

The shock, the guilt, the shame...the *fear*. His mother had been frightened. Of *him*. Of what he might have seen, or heard. And in his entire life he never wanted to see someone look at him with that same fear.

Pietro had arrived and quietly dismissed all the staff. He'd taken his mother into another room and spoken to her for nearly half an hour before he came out. He'd told Santo that he'd called the police and would speak to them himself, that Santo didn't have to worry about anything.

Santo had watched as Pietro managed the entire situation while he'd been unable to take his gaze away from the dead stare of his father's eyes. In the weeks and months that had followed, Pietro was the only person who could get his mother to leave her bed. It hadn't mattered how much he'd begged or pleaded, only Pietro could help.

At sixteen, it hadn't even crossed Santo's mind to be jealous of Pietro. He'd just been unspeakably thankful that there was someone in his mother's life who made her return to even the smallest semblance of the mother he'd once had.

Pietro had tried to explain to him that it had been an accident. That they'd been arguing and that his mother had acted in self-defence. But the older man didn't seem to understand that it didn't matter to Santo. Truly. Self-defence or otherwise. If it hadn't happened like that, it could have been his mother lying at the bottom of the stairs. It was that simple.

But of all the people in his parents' lives, of all the people *here*, it was only an outsider like Pietro who had ever cared about them beyond his father. Pietro, a man who had been born on the wrong side of the tracks and, no matter how much money he'd amassed, would never have gained entry into a society like this. Pedigree. That was what mattered to the people here.

And it turned his stomach.

Someone barged into his shoulder as they passed, Santo's head snapping to follow the blond head back towards the dance area, where various people were gathered. The head turned enough for him to recognise Antony Fairchild's sneer, the foolish boy believing himself to have scored a point on whatever childish game he played in his head.

'He still hasn't forgiven you for snubbing him last year, I see,' commented the richly accented Marie-Laure.

'But have you?' Santo asked in response, without taking his eyes off the boy until he disappeared into the middle of the throng. Santo knew that she was still displeased with him for turning down her advances. And the woman certainly knew how to hold a grudge.

Marie-Laure waited until she had his attention before answering. And he respected that. Whatever could be said about her indiscretions, or her political power plays, Santo always knew where he stood with her. There was artifice about everyone else, but at least with her he knew where he stood.

'That depends.'

'On?' he said, turning his full attention on her. He was standing close enough to see the way her body responded to him instinctively, the widening of her pupils, the almost imperceptible hitch in her breathing.

'How you're planning to make it up to me,' she teased. He smirked.

This was easy. *This* was what he wanted from life. He'd paid his dues with complexities and lies. He didn't need Eleanor or anyone like her. *This* was all he needed.

He bent his lips to her ears. 'Long,' he whispered. 'And slow.' He dipped his head lower. 'And hard,' he promised.

As Eleanor paused on the dance floor the room continued to spin. Frowning, she put her hand to her head, but that didn't help. But what did a little spinning matter when her entire life was spinning out of her control?

She shrugged and smiled at Ekaterina, who had at least stopped asking her if she was okay. She saw Dilly pass by at the edge of the crowd and growled in her mind. Or at least she thought it had been in her mind, but the way people had turned to look at her made her question whether it might have slipped out.

She lurched towards a passing waiter, who looked worried as she went to grab for another shot glass of sambuca.

She *loved* sambuca. She had decided that it was her very favourite drink. It was sweet and thick and after downing it she didn't care as much. Santo could keep his stinking whisky. She would now only drink sambuca for ever.

But as she put the empty glass back on the waiter's tray she caught Santo standing with Marie-Laure from the corner of her eye. Her stomach clenched involuntarily as she saw Marie-Laure gazing at Santo in a way that left absolutely no doubt as to what she wanted from him.

And that wouldn't have been so bad, had Santo not been leaning into her ear with wicked intent as he looked down at her. It was so markedly different to how he'd looked at her at the end of last year.

This was older, darker, *sexier.*

Burned by the shocking twist of jealousy that pierced her breast at the sight of the naked want in the older woman's gaze, Eleanor averted her eyes. It clearly didn't matter to Marie-Laure that he was twenty years her junior, and it clearly didn't matter to Santo who saw them.

She forced down her jealousy just as someone grabbed her around the waist and pulled her back against him.

'Dance with me,' a familiar voice urged in her ear, pulling her against his crotch as irritation and recognition flashed through her body all at once.

'Get off, Tony,' she said, pushing at his hands. But he didn't let go.

'Come on, Lore, you used to love dancing with me,' Tony insisted, his hands leaving her waist to press against her body in places she didn't want him anywhere near.

'Let me go,' she spat.

'You're just playing hard to get,' he accused, his breath hot against her already feverish skin.

Eleanor twisted in his embrace and slapped him hard, and for a second what she saw in his eyes made her blood freeze. And then, before she could feel scared, she was hit by a wave of nausea and she retched. Tony's expression turned from fury to disgust as he pushed her away and all Eleanor could think was that she needed to get to the bathroom before she threw up.

She pushed people out of the way as she lurched awkwardly away from the ballroom and towards the bathrooms she had seen in the corridor. Shoving open the door, she went straight to the sink and ran the cold water tap. Drinking straight from the stream of water, she swallowed, hoping that it would soothe her churning stomach.

After an eternity the feeling passed and she thrust her hand in the water before pressing the cool dampness against her face and skin, no longer caring about her make-up or anything other than making it stop.

She just wanted it all to stop.

Struck by a wave of loneliness, she sobbed and careened into the cubicle, flicking the lock on the door and sinking to the cool tiles of the thankfully clean floor.

'You're just playing hard to get.'

'No one can know.'

'I let a bastard into my family.'

'You'll never see Frederick ever again.'

Round and round the words went, spinning in waves of nausea and the sickly-sweet concoction of alcohol in her stomach. She just wanted to go to sleep. Perhaps then she might never wake up.

Santo stalked towards the bathroom.

'She's fine, Santo. Leave her.'

Santo didn't spare Marie-Laure a backward glance. Anyone in their right mind would have been able to see that Eleanor Carson was as far from fine as was humanly possible.

He'd let his own ego get in the way of what he was supposed to do, which was to keep an eye on her. Self-recrimination was a familiar stick to beat himself with, but he'd never thought he'd have to feel it with regard to her.

He went to knock on the door when a woman emerged from the bathrooms, just able to stop herself in time before she'd walked smack-bang into him.

'Is there anyone other than Eleanor Carson in there?' he demanded.

The woman shook her head quickly and ducked away from him to scurry off down the corridor.

Santo pushed the door open and found the bathroom empty. Decked out in the style of the late eighteen-hundreds, five sinks in front of five mirrors lined one side of the room and five bathroom stalls the other. Powder pink, pastel blue and gold mouldings around the room suited the pavilion's overall design but did nothing but irritate Santo's alert senses.

'Eleanor,' he growled.

No response.

'I know you're in here, I saw you come in.'

Still no response.

'If you don't let me know that you're okay I'll have to assume that you've drunk yourself into such a stupor, you've passed out and I will start kicking down doors,' he warned.

'Gowwaay...' finally came a rather slurred reply.

'No can do, Princess.'

'Jussst leave me alooone...'

Merda. How could her friends let her get like this? And then he remembered what kind of friends they were and felt the resentment build in him again.

'Open the door, Eleanor,' he commanded. 'Now,'

he warned, pulse pounding until he heard the click of the lock.

He pulled the door open and looked down to find her crumpled on the floor.

His heart yanked, hard.

Pitiable. That was what she looked like, and from the flush of shame on her cheeks she knew it too. Anger began to dissolve as he crouched down to her level.

Questions filled his mind and throat.

'Are you okay?'

'Whassit matter?'

He frowned, struggling to interpret her slurred English. 'Eleanor—'

'Doesn't matter. Not any more.'

And, to his horror, she started to cry.

'I want to go home,' she whimpered.

'Okay. I'll get you home,' he said, pulling her gently into his arms.

'But I can't,' she confessed, tucking her head into his chest as if she could hide from the world.

'Of course you can. I'll take you,' he insisted.

'Don't have a home. Don't have a father. Not any more,' she said, before closing her eyes and seemingly passing out.

'Eleanor—' He shook her gently in his arms, but she didn't rouse.

Alarm spread through Santo's entire being.

'Don't have a father.'

Did she know? Did Edward Carson know? *Cristo*, that changed everything.

Santo was halfway out of the door when he came face

to face with her mother, Analise. She took one look at Eleanor in his arms and gestured for him to follow her.

They drew several curious glances as she led Santo towards the back exit.

'Edward's waiting,' Analise warned and Santo nodded to acknowledge he'd heard.

'He knows?' Santo asked Analise.

'Yes. Since November.'

'Are you okay?'

'No. Not at all.'

'What about Eleanor?' he demanded.

'She'll be okay, if she plays along,' her mother confirmed.

Santo gritted his teeth together and unconsciously tightened his hold on her.

'What do you want me to tell Pietro?' he asked.

There was an almost imperceptible hitch in her stride before the words, 'Tell him whatever you want,' were tossed over her shoulder.

As they came out into the slap of cold night air, Eleanor stirred in his arms. He followed Analise Carson to where a black limousine waited, with Edward Carson glaring angrily at him and his wife, yet not even bothering to spare his daughter a glance.

'If you've touched her, I don't want her,' Carson stated.

The accusation hit Santo low and hard, everything primal in him rising against delivering Eleanor back into the man's care.

'If I'd touched her she wouldn't be coming back to you,' Santo growled and he knew in that moment it was the truth. If Eleanor ever came to him she would never need anything from Edward Carson again. He would give her whatever she needed for however long she needed it.

'Put her in the car,' Carson ordered and he looked to Eleanor's mother for permission. All she had to do was say no and he would take her away.

He could see the warring in her gaze and he knew what was holding both women back. Frederick. Eleanor's brother.

Fighting every instinct he had, Santo put Eleanor gently into the car and watched as Carson slammed the door and went round to the other side of the limousine, not taking his eyes off Santo until the last second.

As Santo watched the car disappear into the night he retrieved his phone and found Pietro's name.

'Carson knows,' Santo said the moment the call clicked through. 'As does Eleanor.'

The silence on the end of the phone was deafening.

The rules of the game had now changed.

CHAPTER SIX

New Year's Eve four years ago, Prague

FIREWORKS EXPLODED ACROSS Prague's Old Town Square. In the distance, the fourteenth century church stared down at the hundreds of thousands of people cramming themselves onto its streets, each as eager as the next to count down the New Year by one of the oldest medieval astronomical clocks in the world.

The mishmash of old architectural styles, statues and memorials stood firm against wave after wave of tourists and locals alike, each entertained by the ferocious fireworks that exploded nearly at eye level, causing fear and delight in worryingly equal measure. Santo looked out upon them all, separated by a pane of thick glass, wondering what he would do with this one night a year if he had the freedom to choose for himself.

'I wasn't sure you'd come this year,' said Mads Rassmussen.

Santo gave him a death stare. For nearly twelve months, rather than the literal fires he had fought in previous years across his olive groves in Puglia, he had been defending himself against financial attack from not just one but two different sides, Edward Carson on one and Marie-Laure on the other.

Mads laughed. 'You have nothing to fear from me, Sabatini. And besides, I've enough on my hands with Rassmuss Technologies to worry about olive groves. But I did hear a rumour that you might be interested in renewable—'

'No idea what you're talking about,' Santo replied, cutting off the young Scandinavian before he could finish his sentence. A flash of concern rushed painfully through his body. The number of people who knew about his business interest in renewable energies could be counted on less than one hand. It was certainly something he didn't want anyone here to know about.

'Relax. When you're ready, let me know and I promise it will go no further,' Mads said, a business card palmed into Santo's hand with a shake.

Santo waited until the other man had joined his father and some others before looking at the handwritten mobile number on the blank card with the initials MR embossed in the corner. He barely restrained himself from laughing at this silly game of cloak and dagger but, after the year he'd had, he understood the need for it—and appreciated Rassmussen's understanding of that more than he'd care to admit.

Santo had expected Carson's underhand tactics, Pietro and he had all but prepared for it, but when Marie-Laure had decided to use her investments to take out her frustration and resentment at his abandonment of her last year, it had forced him to split his focus and his business had suffered.

It had suffered because of Eleanor.

But that wasn't why he was ignoring her increasingly desperate attempts to snare his attention from across the room. Steeling himself, he turned in the opposite direction, making his way to the bar of the old banquet hall acquired by the Svobodas for the evening. They must have booked it several years in advance; every window along the entire length of the hall had a view of the clock tower. But, no matter how much he tried to shake her off, she consumed his thoughts entirely.

Resentment and frustration reinforced his determination to keep her at arm's length. He had never argued with Pietro before this year. Not once had they exchanged anything more than support and encouragement. But Santo's feelings for Eleanor had become much more complex than simple attraction, and he'd struggled with Pietro's decision to maintain the fragile status quo. Their heated exchange had made Santo feel as if he were both disappointing Pietro and himself at the same time. As if neither could win because neither was wrong. But with the disconcerting feeling that neither was right either.

Santo might have disagreed with Pietro's decision, but he respected the man completely. And what was the alternative? Eleanor would hardly come to him, leaving her brother and her mother behind under Edward's control. The helplessness of the situation ate at him and his sense of control in a way he disliked intensely.

And the difficulty he had in leashing his wants beneath the yoke of his word was enough to warn him of just how dangerous she had become to him. Almost as dangerous as he was to her. But his decision to keep distance between them seemed to make her only more desperate to seek him out.

Santo was no stranger to the feeling that eyes were on him. Edward had thrown a few daggers his way upon entry, which was only to be expected. That Santo had managed to slip out from the financial chokehold Edward had tried to get him in was a source of great amusement to some, and consternation to Carson and his supporters. Edward had moved too fast and too hard and had lost himself, and them, a significant chunk of money. But it had cost Santo personally. He'd had to pull his funding from the project he'd been working on in secret to do so and set himself back maybe three or so years. And that hurt.

As Santo moved through the various groups discussing their business interests, he kept his gaze purposely away from the Carsons. The less they interacted, the better for everyone concerned. But he could almost feel Edward's attention being turned to him by his daughter's behaviour.

Cristo. Hadn't she learned anything from last year? he thought angrily, reluctantly realising that there was only one way that this would end, as he turned on his heel and stalked from the room.

He barely saw any of the grandeur of the old banquet hall as he entered the hallway, from which various private rooms led. And while there were nearly two hundred people in attendance that evening, he was painfully aware that only one tailed him down that corridor. Barely restraining a growl, he shoved open a door and shut it behind him, hoping that Eleanor Carson wasn't so stupid as to follow him in here.

Eleanor wanted to know why he was ignoring her. Needed it like a feral thing in her blood.

All evening she'd hoped to snare his attention but had failed, again and again. At first, she'd simply wanted to thank him for last year. Again. Over the year, she'd come to think of him as her knight in matt black armour. Santo certainly had none of the shine and pomp of fairy tale heroes. But what use did she have for them? No, she needed the brutal honesty he offered.

But when she'd realised that he was ignoring her on purpose she'd been devastated...until that had turned to anger. She had been shocked by the fury that had whipped through her like wildfire. She'd almost had to physically hold herself back from going up to him and demanding why.

She knew it was dangerous to speak to him, it would draw her fa—*Edward's* ire. More of it, anyway. She clenched her jaw, hoping that the tension would hold her still enough to stop her from looking his way. She knew they were by the bar set up along the back wall of the hall, speaking to the Müllers.

Her mother would be standing beside him, Eleanor imagined, wondering if anyone would notice the paleness of her skin beneath the make-up, or the brittle way she held herself. Fragile, breakable, fractured—most definitely—but not yet broken, Eleanor thought of her mother.

But the lies that lay between the three of them were like splinters stuck under the skin, festering, infected, untreated.

She'd thought that the worst thing had happened to her when she'd discovered that Edward wasn't her father. But when she'd finally emerged from her room after the drunken disaster of last New Year's Eve she'd found out the true extent of her situation.

Her grades at university had slipped under the strain of her personal life and Edward had decided that funding any future studies was a waste of his finances, so he had cancelled them. He had put a block on her cards and her account and finally she had realised how much of her life was under his control. Any attempt to circumvent his authority was met with the reminder that he would take Freddie and leave. Her mother's desperate urging for her to do as he said only damaged what was left of her soul that bit more.

And standing in the grand banquet hall overlooking the cobbled streets of this beautiful, ancient European city, she'd just wanted someone who wouldn't make her feel like a stranger in her own body. She'd wanted Santo. But he had cut her dead. It was the final straw and she barely cared whether Edward saw or not, as she followed him out of the hall and into the corridor.

With all the hurts and denigrations and misery she'd had to suffer this last year riding her hard, at that point it wouldn't have even mattered if he'd gone straight to the men's toilets, she would have followed him. A red haze had descended and even if distantly she could see that she was skirting the edge of hysteria...it didn't matter. It was too late.

She turned the handle on the door she'd seen Santo disappear behind and pushed.

Barely half a step across the threshold and a hand snatched around her wrist and she was dragged into the room, the door slammed behind her, and she found herself pushed up against it, staring into the furious depths of Santo Sabatini's unfathomable gaze.

'Who do you think you are playing with?' he demanded.

'Wh-wh-what?' she asked, everything in her—all the anger, the edge of hysteria, the determination—retreating under the sheer force of *him*. He crowded her, the press of his body oddly delicious to her near delirious state, his piercing aquamarine gaze flashing shards of ice that burned where they fell as he took in her every response.

Life. Her body had come to life for the first time that entire year.

She was touch-starved, and her body responded to his as if it were food. She wanted to gorge on him. Worse. She wanted him to gorge on *her*. To feast on her. To take everything that remained of her and leave nothing behind.

'Little girl, do not mess with me,' he warned, his voice a growl that sent shivers down her body to parts of her she'd been utterly unaware of until that moment. It called to her in a deep, primal way—the challenge, the dare, the taunt from him.

She had been dismissed, rejected, cast aside by almost everyone. Even him, and she was so damn tired of it.

'Then stop messing with *me*,' she stressed, pushing

herself away from the door and walking him back further into the room. 'Why are you ignoring me?' she demanded.

'Why are you looking for me?' he retaliated, his question, his tone throwing her off-course.

She clenched her teeth together. 'I was looking for you because I thought you were different,' she accused.

'Don't you dare compare me to them,' he threw back at her almost before the words had left her lips. The slash of his hand through the air punctuated his response, his fury feeding her own.

'Why not? You're here every year, just like them. Your business is financed through investments in their companies and they invest in yours. You keep yourself pleasured with their wives,' she lashed out, her eyes narrow and the seething anger that she wasn't able to unleash *anywhere* else, here suddenly free to roam. It rose within her like a fire-breathing monster, consuming everything in its path.

'Jealousy? It doesn't suit you, *cara*,' he all but snarled at her.

'I'm not jealous of a widow nearly twice my age,' she lied. Because she was. Because Santo had looked at Marie-Laure in a way that he'd never looked at her. And she wanted that. She wanted something, anything other than the near violent fury that threatened to tear her sanity from her.

He frowned, just for a moment, as if he'd read her thoughts. As if she'd let them slip from the locked box she kept them in all year round.

'You should go before someone finds you in here,' he

said, turning his back on her and once again dismissing her from his company.

Go here. Stay there. Don't do that. Do this.

He was just like Edward. Ordering her around as if what she wanted, what she felt, had absolutely no importance to them.

'No,' she replied stubbornly. 'I won't.'

'Fine. If you insist on behaving like a child, *I'll* go.'

'Don't you dare,' she warned, moving to stand in his way.

Santo barked out a mean laugh. 'Why? What are you going to do? Stop me?' he demanded and made to push past her, but she moved to block his path.

Muscle clenching at his jaw, Santo could feel the anger in her pulsing from her in waves. But it was more complex than pure anger—something he was intimately familiar with. He could sense her helpless frustration, confusion, hurt... Arousal.

Cristo, she didn't know what she was doing to him, he thought as he looked away.

She didn't know how much *he* felt, as he wrestled with his own frustration and anger, his own confusion. They were both breathing hard, as if they were fighting battles and demons that demanded their all.

'What do you *want*, Eleanor?' he growled, hoping to scare her off, hoping to send her running back to the safety of the party. Back to someone else.

'I want you to kiss me,' she said. 'Like you kiss *her*.'

A ripcord was wrenched within him, suspending him in mid-air on a piece of string tied right to her.

'What?' he asked, half convinced he'd imagined her words.

'I want you to kiss me like you kiss her,' Eleanor repeated, the dark gleam in her eyes swallowing the innocence whole.

Her tone left no doubt about whom she was speaking. Eleanor must have seen them last year. *Merda*, she didn't even realise that she was the reason that nothing had happened between him and Marie-Laure. And that nothing would ever happen again.

And here Eleanor was, with that awful question on her lips. Couldn't she tell how different they were? Couldn't she see?

'No,' he bit out through clenched teeth. 'I can't do that.'

'Then what use are you to me?' she said, shoving back at him.

The taunt, the accusation, cut too close to the bone after years of stepping back and forth up to this line— the line that he couldn't, shouldn't, cross. Ever.

'You want to use me?' he demanded, stepping closer to her, crowding her a little more, letting just a little of his own anger loose.

'No, I want you to use *me*,' she cried, stepping forward, closing the distance between them until they were head to head, more like enemies than potential lovers.

'You want me to be just like all the other men in your life, do you?' he demanded, sick to his stomach.

'No, I want you to do what I want, on my terms,' she cried. 'Because I *want* this. I want to feel anything other than abandoned, rejected, unworthy, unloved and unknown.' Each of these descriptions of herself twisted the knife in his chest. But then her eyes darkened.

'And if you're not going to help me, then I'll find someone who will,' she threatened, turning on her heel as if to leave.

His hand snaked out and slipped around her waist, pulling her back against his chest with gentle force. Fast breaths expanded her ribcage, flexing against his arm, tension holding her stiff in his arms as if she wasn't sure whether she wanted to move or not, the scent of her rising from the curve of her neck and striking him deeply. Irrevocably.

He could lie to himself and dress it up a million different ways. But what really hid beneath the layers of protest and objection—towards her, the situation, the consequences that Eleanor Carson seemed wholly ignorant of—was that he had never, not once, been able to stop thinking about her…about the way she had looked up at him that night in Berlin. The way she had dared him to kiss her.

The way he'd wanted to, like nothing he'd ever experienced before in his life. The way he'd been tempted to throw away his promise to Pietro. The way he'd wanted to throw away everything he knew about himself and how devastatingly close he could be to his father sometimes and take what he wanted. It had nearly broken him and she'd had no idea. And here she was, threatening to find someone else to satisfy the same craving that coursed through his veins like a curse. And as she arched into his hold, her hands wrapping around the arms that held her tight, her backside restlessly pressing against his crotch, the last fragile tie to his sanity broke.

He spun her in his arms and her eager mouth met his in an almost violent confrontation. Tongues teased, teeth clashed, but it was her half-cried moan of sheer arousal that cut him off at the knees.

Santo pulled her tight against the length of his body, the hard ridge of his need for her pressing against her core. Unable to restrain himself, he felt feral, animal-istic, primal and raw, in a way he'd *never* experienced before in his life. It was as if all their anger, all their frustration, all their hopelessness was bleeding out into their passion and he could only hope that it would run dry and leave him spent enough to let her go when it was done.

Eleanor pulled him against her by the lapels of his jacket, and he let himself be led straight into the drug that was Eleanor Carson. The boldness of her tongue had taken him by surprise and he was insatiable, addicted, unable to stop himself from going back for more... Dammit, for everything and anything he could get.

His pulse raged beyond his control, need a stronger impulse than his desire to breathe. She was pushing him closer and closer to the same hot-headed insanity of his father...and that alone was enough to make him sever the kiss.

He pulled back, breathing as if he'd run a marathon, the struggle to get himself back under control alarm-ingly close to a limit he rarely tested.

'Why are you doing this?' he demanded on a shaky inhale, his forehead pressed against hers, his eyes closed, half-hopeful and half-fearful of what he might see in the espresso rich depths of her eyes.

'Because I have nothing left to lose,' she whispered against his lips as if it were some great confession.

Santo hadn't realised he'd been holding his breath until it whooshed, hot and hard and heavy—and devastated.

Her words had broken something inside him and he let her go from where he'd been holding her with numb fingers and turned, his back to her, while he gathered himself.

He shook his head. He should have known better. He should have realised. Oh, she probably hadn't meant to be so cruel. But her words still cut him like a knife. She was only here, only asking that of him because she had reached the bottom of the barrel. She was only here because it was about *her*.

Had she still been the darling daughter of Edward Carson there was no way she'd have been standing here, begging him to kiss her. She'd have got as close to the flame as she could before running back to her friends with a near-scandal she could titillate and delight them with, without ever once having got her hands dirty. Because that was what she saw him as—playing in the dirt. She could walk away from him and wash her hands clean.

Oh, he had sympathy with her plight. But only to an extent. Because when *his* world had fallen apart he'd not had the luxury of buckling. He'd not had the opportunity to be self-indulgent and drink himself into a stupor, or act out like a child. No, he'd had to assume control of the Sabatini Group, and within months of his father's death he was standing head-to-head with some of the men in this room who would have taken his company from him. Almost every day for nearly three years he'd had eyewatering, heart-stopping buyout packages. The kind that would have erased an entire country's debt. And what was Eleanor doing? Dropping out of university and trying to lose herself in mindless hookups.

'You don't get it, do you?' he sneered, returning to her words. Her self-pity, her self-absorption, burying the sharp sting of hurt beneath frustration and anger.

She looked back at him, wide-eyed and confused.

'You're such a child,' he continued remorselessly. 'You *always* have more to lose. If you have no care for yourself, then what about your mother? What about your brother? Or has it not even occurred to you that Edward could be using you against *them*?'

'Y-you know?' Eleanor reeled back in shock as if she'd been slapped.

But she hadn't. She'd just been told the truth, Santo thought grimly as he followed her back into the room. Something that had clearly been denied her far too long. And it had done her absolutely no good whatsoever.

'Yes, I know,' he confessed. 'You said as much last year before I returned you to your mother.'

'You can't tell anyone,' she begged.

A single bitter laugh burst from him. 'Do you not think I would have done so by now, were I going to? Oh, not for you. And not because Carson hasn't been trying to tank my business for the last twelve months. Your mother deserves *none* of this.'

Eleanor shook her pretty head, as if to try and both deny and assimilate what he was saying at the same time. Santo bit back a curse at the way she had paled.

'Sit down, before you fall down,' he ordered, ushering her towards a chair, before walking over to a glass-fronted drinks cabinet.

He reached for the whisky and retrieved two glasses from the backlit glass shelf. This was clearly some kind of after-dinner retirement room and had everything one would need. The décor was rich forest greens and golds and burgundy reds, so dark and so different from his own taste. And suddenly he just wanted to be home in his villa in Puglia, nestled in the olive groves beneath the heat of the sun and the simplicity of the landscape around him.

He was damn tired of all the politics and manipulation, the bribery and secrets and retaliations for perceived or real slights. He wanted to be away from it all. Including *her*.

He turned back to find Eleanor staring ahead as if in shock.

'I hadn't...' She paused, cleared her throat and tried again. 'I hadn't thought of it like that,' she confessed, as if ashamed.

He went to where she sat in the chair and passed her the glass, before going to stand by the window as far away from her as he could get.

'Every single thing I thought I knew about my life was untrue,' she said, as if putting her thoughts into words for the first time. 'And I don't know what that makes me,' she said sadly. 'I don't know who I am.'

And wasn't that the difference between them? Santo had never had the luxury of the lie—he had always known the terror and fear of his father, the false smiles of people who would never help his mother or him, but only profit from their silence. He had always known who he was: the son of a violent, selfish bastard. Santo had inherited his genes, his blood, and always had to be watchful for when those characteristics would appear, when that anger would finally take hold and he would break the things most precious to him. Like father, like son. And the only way to ensure that he didn't inflict that kind of hurt on the people he loved was simple. Don't love.

Eleanor's fingers gripped the seat of the chair as her head spun. A distant part of her thought she should be used to this by now. But she wasn't.

Santo's kiss had been one thing—spectacular. A short-lived moment of ecstasy she could never have imagined. That rush of all that she had felt had thrust her to the very brink of what she'd thought she'd always wanted. Before she had dashed them both on the rocks with her thoughtless words.

She had realised her mistake almost the moment the words were out of her mouth. Guilt coloured her cheeks. She had asked him to use her, but she was the one using him. Tonight. Maybe last year and the year before that too. Shame coursed through her blood, thick, heavy and hot, and she deserved every minute of discomfort it brought her.

'I'm sorry, you didn't deserve—'

'What I deserve or don't deserve is nothing to do with you. You asked for a kiss. You got what you asked for.'

Eleanor paled beneath the realisation of the truth of his accusation. She *had* been behaving like a child, thinking only of how the situation had affected her.

She nodded and, leaving the glass of whisky he had offered her untouched, stood.

Her head swam a little and she wanted air. Fresh air. She needed to think. She couldn't afford to be so selfish. She couldn't afford to behave like a child. She couldn't afford to keep hurting the people around her: her mother, her brother... *Santo*.

Raising a shaking hand to her lips, she knew that no matter who she kissed, or how many people, none would stand up to what she had felt with Santo.

'I—'

'You should leave. Now,' he commanded, deliberately turning his back to her, and she knew that it was the end of the discussion. It hurt, but she'd done it to herself and it was time that she owned that.

But as she left the room she could only wish that her selfishness hadn't cost her *him*.

CHAPTER SEVEN

New Year's Eve three years ago, Barcelona

ELEANOR LOOKED OUT beyond the bustling lights glowing from the Port of Barcelona, even on this night, to the dark blank space of the Balearic Sea, wondering if she could count the ways that her life had changed again.

Santo wouldn't know it, but what had passed between them last year had altered her fundamentally. In rare moments she thought that he might have said what he did because she'd hurt him. But then she came to her senses, refusing to overestimate her importance to him. Whatever had caused them, his words had been blunt and forceful to the point of bruising, but she had desperately needed to hear them.

And from the moment that she'd returned home she'd known that she needed to make serious changes in both her behaviour and her mindset. Shame and embarrassment at how selfish she had been were only useful if they drove her to do better. So that was what she'd made them do. Drive her forward.

At home, when Freddie was back from boarding school she had spent as much time with him as she could. She had soaked in all that he was, hoping that he would some day realise how much she loved him, and how much she'd tried to protect him from Edward—who was unable to separate them without making an unnecessary scene.

And with her mother, Eleanor had tried her hardest to make peace with what little relationship they had under Edward's watchful eye. Although it seemed paranoid, she couldn't help but feel that the staff had been instructed to report back any conversations she shared with her mother, and the newly increased number of them meant that there was very little time for them to be alone.

She'd reached out to her university professor and had arranged to repeat the last year through remote learning. She'd been able to take out a personal loan to cover the tuition fees, whilst also securing a job at Mads Rassmussen's London office.

Edward hadn't liked that one little bit, but she'd sold it to him that it would enable her to keep an ear to the ground about the financial goings-on of one of the families. She doubted that Edward believed a word she'd said, but he'd surprisingly let it go.

But between the full-time job, her studies and trying to keep a fragile peace at home, Eleanor was feeling the strain. Strain that she pushed down hard. Other people had been through worse. She'd had twenty years of privileged pampering. She would certainly survive the next few years. All she had to do was wait until Freddie was eighteen, and the three of them could leave. Until then, Eleanor would do everything she could to ensure that they had somewhere to go and some money to take with them. They didn't even need that much. Just enough. Enough *never* to be dependent on someone else ever again.

'Ah, here she is, my latest employee,' announced Mads with Ekaterina on his arm.

Eleanor smiled warmly at the couple. While she worked hard to keep her guard up around them, about what she said of herself and her family, she liked them. And God knew, she would have been nowhere without Mads taking a risk on a woman with no work history, no experience and no degree to her name.

'How is it, working for Mads? Is he a mean boss?' Kat asked, poking her fiancé teasingly.

'Terrible,' Eleanor replied with mock horror. 'He even makes me work on Fridays,' she replied.

'You can't make her do that.' Kat turned to him, outraged.

'My love, *most* people who are employed have to work on Fridays,' he chided.

A part of Eleanor was amazed at how clueless Ekaterina was, but the other part was sympathetic. Just remembering the sheer basic day-to-day things that she hadn't known when she'd first started work filled Eleanor with deep embarrassment.

It had been hard to win over her fellow staff members, all of whom—understandably—thought she was only 'playing' at having a job. The first few months as a personal assistant had been truly awful for her. But every day she went back, every time she worked a little longer, a little harder, she won another inch of their respect. Eventually she'd picked up the basic skills that she lacked and was able to add that to the foundation from her university degree and she had finally found her feet.

Eleanor gritted her teeth as Dilly passed by, her slow head-to-toe perusal making it clear that her one-time friend had recognised the dress that Eleanor had worn before at a previous event. The mean tittering from Dilly and another girl told her that it wouldn't be long before whatever rumour the other woman had spun it into would be around the room in no time.

Well, let them. Eleanor no longer had the luxury of wasting money on brand-new gowns. And while the income she had saved that year was almost embarrassingly low, in some ways it was more than she could ever have imagined. It was *hers*. She'd earnt it. Herself. It hadn't been given to her and couldn't be taken away. And that made her feel like it was millions.

'Well, Thompson has been saying how good you've been getting on in the last few months, so keep it up!' Mads said, with a little fist pump that made her smile.

When she'd first approached him she knew that he had been both suspicious and surprised. She'd told him only as much as she'd dared. He'd taken such a chance on her, and she'd never forget it.

'Uh-oh,' Kat said, leaning in to whisper. 'Grumpy is here. And it seems he's not alone,' she added.

Eleanor frowned and turned to see who had just entered the room.

She masked her expression the moment she saw him, not wanting a single reflection of the impact he made on her to show. Not wanting anyone to guess that the moment she'd seen him it had felt as if the air had been sucked from her lungs. As if time had stopped the beat of her heart.

Standing nearly a foot taller than almost everyone else, he insolently surveyed the room. Thick, dark hair, effortlessly styled; his hands had run through the wet strands, with maybe the slightest slick of gel, she imagined. A rich olive tan graced his skin, presumably from his time outside amongst the olive groves.

Eleanor's cheeks flushed. In the brief moments she had to herself, away from work or studies, she had pored over any news about him she could find.

From where she stood, his face side on to her, she couldn't see, but could well remember, the scar he'd confessed was inflicted by his father. And yet she couldn't help but wonder at the invisible ones he bore, where no one could see them, or reach them to heal.

Santo turned to the doorway and smiled, the expression completely changing his face. The stern lines that defined him eased and he looked a little younger, he looked softer, without undermining the powerful impact he made. He reached out his hand and Eleanor followed the line of his arm to see a young woman emerge from the doorway.

She pressed her lips together to stop the gasp of hurt from escaping. Because the way that Santo looked at the young, dark-haired woman was nothing she'd ever seen from him before.

Just as he returned his gaze to the room, Eleanor shifted so that her back was to them, desperately hoping that

Santo hadn't caught her staring. After what had passed between them last year, she wanted to avoid him at all costs.

Santo held his arm out to Amita. The new stepdaughter of one of the few men here he could almost bring himself to respect, Santo had promised to accompany her to her first New Year's Eve party. Karl Ivanov's investments in the Sabatini Group were largely silent, making him one of the easier investors to deal with. But also Santo appreciated that the man didn't get into any of the backbiting and backstabbing that most of the others seemed to delight in.

Amita was a nice girl, but timid. Her stepfather was right to be worried. Originally from Jaipur, her whole sheltered world had been uprooted dramatically and Karl was incredibly concerned about her.

Despite the clear and very platonic understanding between him and Amita, she'd clung to him like a limpet from the moment they'd entered the room. He could feel the curious gazes they'd attracted and when Karl and Amita's mother, Aditi, joined them the whispers grew to an almost audible level.

'They're going to think we're together,' whispered Amita for his ears only.

'Let them. It doesn't matter,' he replied sincerely.

In fact, after the last few years, it was probably a good thing that people here thought that he was 'off the market'. Carson's blows had lessened, having presumably found bigger fish to fry, and Marie-Laure had found herself a new plaything. He was hardly surprised that the rumour mill had named Antony Fairchild as her new lover.

Poor bastard didn't know what he was in for.

As Santo led her towards their table in the Casa Llotja de Mar, he was impressed by the space. White and black squares covered the floor like a chequerboard, but it was the huge stone arches that drew the gaze to the dizzying height of the ceiling. A first-floor balcony wrapped around the magnificent room, and a smile caught his lips when he heard Amita gasp.

'It's so beautiful.'

'Mmm,' he replied noncommittally.

The white-clothed, perfectly dressed tables waiting for the promised eight-course meal that evening hugged the edges of the space, leaving the centre of the room free for those standing and chatting or even dancing a little.

As he took his seat, he kept his gaze firmly on his companions and away from where he knew Eleanor Carson would be found. He had absolutely no intention of running into her tonight.

He was here, keeping his promise, he just didn't have to interact with her personally.

Which was precisely why he'd asked Mads Rassmussen to dangle himself enticingly as a prospective boss for her. Santo had killed two birds with the same stone—created a way to keep an eye on Eleanor without getting directly involved, in exchange for working with Rassmussen on the side project he'd resumed after rectifying the damage done the year before.

Pietro hadn't been overjoyed by the news of what she

was doing, but his hands were still firmly tied. Watching the old man's helplessness had been...difficult for Santo. He'd been a mentor, a father figure, representing authority and security. But Eleanor was making the man weak, making him vulnerable, and Santo didn't like that one bit.

She was a thorn in both their sides and he wanted her gone.

But, no matter what he wanted, his body had different ideas. Torturing him with erotic images at night, with memories during the day, with awareness of her right here, right now. Fingers tripped across his skin, beneath his shirt, gripping him in places that made him damn thankful he was sitting down at the table.

'Do you two want to go and mingle before we eat?' Aditi asked, her accent inflecting her words in a pleasant way.

Amita shook her head, and Santo nodded that it was fine to stay at the table. Aditi's smile was enough to tell him how important this was to her. He should tell Karl to get them both away from here and never come back. But Karl had enough of both clout and charm to make himself unthreatening to others, so Santo was sure that they would be fine.

As the waiter passed, he and Karl removed the bottles of wine from the table.

'You can drink,' Amita assured him.

'That's okay, I'm happy not to,' he explained, the gratefulness in her answering gaze more than he deserved. He'd already decided that he was done drinking around this lot.

He had warned Eleanor last year about growing up and taking things seriously. It was time that he did the same.

As Karl, Amita and Aditi fell into easy conversation, Santo's mind was elsewhere. One of the largest neighbouring competitors for olive oil in Puglia had approached him last week, needing to sell the company. The man's brother-in-law had got into gambling debt with some very dangerous people and he needed capital fast. Others had come sniffing around, but the man wanted to sell to Santo because he respected the land and the local community.

Santo knew that everyone here thought he'd made his millions by being ruthless. Not a single one of them would have considered that one could make money and still keep one's morals. The work he'd done in the past years to create a community response to the fires that had ravaged Puglia and, in all likelihood would continue to do so in the future, had garnered respect. And that had paid dividends.

His phone rang and, excusing himself from the table, he left to find a quiet place to take the call.

He followed the staircase behind him up to the second-floor balcony, the lighting dim and the noise much quieter up here. It was a quick call, barely a few words, and just like that, Santo had nearly doubled the size of his estate.

Pocketing his phone, he braced his elbows on the railing and surveyed the scene below. People were chatting, dancing, laughing and drinking and all he could think was that a man's entire career, his life, had just been surrendered.

A movement further along the balcony caught his eye and he'd barely turned when recognition struck him hard. *Of course* it would be her. *Of course* they would have somehow found each other amongst the two hundred guests that evening.

Eleanor wanted to hide but she knew he'd seen her. He hadn't at first, not when he'd been on the phone, but in trying to leave she'd made herself known.

'I'm sorry, I didn't mean to interrupt.'

She felt the pause between her statement and his response like an eternity.

'Nothing to interrupt.' The clipped words dropped to the floor between them like a stone.

She nodded, deeply uncomfortable with the seething twist of self-pity and jealousy coursing through her veins. It shouldn't matter. She could be happy for him. Because, truly, he deserved to be happy.

'I...' She let the sentence trail off as she saw he'd turned away, but the word stopped him.

Eventually he looked back at her. *'Sì?'*

'It's okay,' she said, gesturing for him to leave.

Santo bit out an irritable sigh. 'What is it, Eleanor?'

She swallowed. 'I just wanted you to know that I heard what you said last year,' she explained, staring at the floor, cursing herself for being so weak. He'd told her to be strong. To be stronger. And she wanted to show him that she *was*. 'I...have made some changes this year and I...just wanted you to know that,' she said, raising her eyes to his face before the overwhelming urge to turn back into the shadows and disappear crashed over her.

He stared back at her, the blankness painful, but nothing more than she deserved. She had used him last year. And instinctively she knew that few people did that and survived unscathed.

'Did you want an award? A round of applause, perhaps?'

'No, I just wanted you to know,' she said, holding fast against the disdain she saw in his gaze. But disdain was better than what had been there before, which was nothing less than a brutal indifference. 'I have a job now. And I'm finishing my degree. I have a plan,' she said, determined for the first time that evening. To prove herself to him, to herself even.

He frowned for the first time, the tiny movement showing that he wasn't just a statue.

'What plan?' he asked.

She shook her head. 'It's not important,' she said, suddenly feeling the urge to run. She went to push past him on the shallow balcony, but he caught her upper arm in his hand.

'What plan, Eleanor?' he asked again, more forcefully.

'It's nothing,' she dismissed. 'Certainly nothing to do with you,' she said, confused by the sudden whiplash of his interest.

'Carson is not a man to mess with,' Santo warned.

Eleanor let out a surprised laugh. 'You think I don't know that?'

'Whatever you're thinking—'

'Is none of your business, as I've said,' she stressed, getting annoyed. Yes, he'd helped her see what a mess she'd been making of things, but that didn't mean he got to treat her like a child.

She pulled her arm back and, as if only because he didn't want to make a scene, he released her.

'Don't do anything stupid, Eleanor,' he commanded.

She wanted to rail against the accusation, but the problem was, she had earned it. He had seen her passed out drunk. He had experienced her misguided attempts to lose herself in *him*. He had every right to believe that she would do something stupid.

And, just like that, any anger or indignation at his tone evaporated.

'I won't,' she replied sincerely. If she had learned anything about Edward it was that the man was fiercely intelligent. And she would have to be more so.

'But I really don't want any bad blood between us,' she admitted, seeking for a sense of the control and calm that she had heavily relied on throughout this year. 'I sincerely apologise for any offence I caused last year. I wasn't...' I wasn't *okay*, she wanted to confess. The last time she'd seen him, she'd been so very bleak. 'I wasn't quite myself,' was all she could admit to.

She swallowed, looking once again at the floor, un-able—no, *unwilling*—to meet his gaze.

There was a pause.

'And you are now?' came the enquiry.

She bit the inside of her cheek. In truth, probably not

completely, but he didn't need to know that. She nodded instead, not wanting to lie to him.

Santo peered at her through the gentle downlighting of the balcony. He wasn't sure he believed her. In fact, when he'd first taken a look at her—a proper look—he'd been surprised, and not in a good way.

She had lost weight since last year. Quite a bit, and she hadn't had all that much to lose in the first place. There was a dark smudge beneath each eye that was still visible through her make-up. And he recalled earlier having heard some mean gossip about her wearing a dress she'd been seen in before.

The grey dress served only to make her look even more pale than usual, he thought. He cursed himself for being mean. She was clearly suffering in one way or another.

Some protector he was, he thought, viciously chastising himself.

'If there's something I can do,' he offered lamely, knowing with absolute conviction that she would never turn to him for help. No. Her pride—which he respected—wouldn't allow that.

She dismissed his offer with a wave of her hand, just as he'd expected, surprised to find that it stung as sharply as a slap.

'Not at all. Things are actually going really well,' she said gamely, her eyes bright. *Too* bright.

Cristo. He had let his ego override the promise he'd made to Pietro, but also what was staring him right in the face. Yes, she might have behaved selfishly, but what should he have expected? She'd grown up pampered, indulged and spoilt. It was a miracle she'd lasted a week at Rassmuss Technologies, let alone eleven months.

He didn't think for a moment that any of her contemporaries would have had even half the fortitude she must have had to still be standing, once Edward had turned against her. How had he not seen that? How had he not recognised that?

Because you let your attraction towards her mess with your mind, his inner voice said.

'If you need anything…' he tried again, but once again she shook him off.

'I'd rather not, actually,' she said, her smile a little more brittle this time. 'I…want to do this on my own.' She nodded, as if to herself. 'It feels good,' she admitted. 'The things I've earned. I've enjoyed it.'

Truth rang loudly in her words and he instinctively knew that this time it wasn't false bravado. She meant what she said.

'I'm pleased,' he replied honestly.

'Actually,' she said, frowning, half hesitant, 'there is one thing you could do for me.' Her hands were twisting in front of her.

Anything, he nearly replied and, not trusting himself to speak, he simply nodded for her to continue.

She bit her lip. 'Could I ask you for a promise?'

The confusion must have shown on his face, because she smiled.

'Don't worry, it shouldn't cost you anything.'

'Money would probably be easier,' he replied without

thinking and where once she might have laughed, now she only smiled awkwardly.

Oh, yes, it was safe to say that Eleanor Carson had very much learned the value of money in the last year.

'Could I ask you to promise never to lie to me?'

He blinked, closing his mouth before it dropped open more than the few millimetres it already had in shock.

Money most definitely *would* have been easier.

How could he make that promise to her? He was already lying to her. Had lied to her every single time they had met. Their entire interactions were coloured by that lie.

But how could he not, when she stared up at him with something in her eyes that he couldn't shatter? So much had been taken from her, could he really afford to take this from her too?

But agreeing to her request would cross a line that he would be unable to reinstate. And a perverse part of him almost welcomed that knowledge. Welcomed the fact that what she was asking from him guaranteed a future in which he would disappoint her. One way or another, it would be a certainty if he gave her his word.

He took a breath, and ignored the way it shuddered in his lungs as he did so.

'Yes, I can promise that,' he said, wondering if by not saying the words it made his crime any less.

The smile that lit her features this time was genuine and warm. She bounced a little on the balls of her feet and he wished it didn't make him want to smile in response.

'Thank you. I wanted at least one person here who

won't lie to me,' she said and, before he could react, she leant forward and reached up to kiss his cheek, his stomach flipping into his throat and his soul going straight to hell.

By the time he had regained control of himself, she had disappeared back down the stairs and off somewhere he couldn't follow. Slowly, step by step, he returned to his place at the table with Karl, Aditi and Amita.

'Is everything okay?' Amita asked.

He forced a smile to his face. 'Yes, in fact I've just acquired a new business.'

'On New Year's Eve?' asked Karl, impressed.

'Yes. A neighbour. I've nearly doubled my land.'

'Now, that really is a reason to celebrate,' Aditi exclaimed.

He nodded, and let them raise their glasses, even though there was no alcohol on the table. And no matter how self-righteous he'd been about the need to keep his head that evening, he would have given his neighbour's business back for a bottle of whisky in that moment.

'Who was that woman?' Amita asked quietly, looking back up to the empty balcony.

'No one important,' he lied for the second time that night.

CHAPTER EIGHT

New Year's Eve two years ago, Amsterdam

THE SOUND OF laughter was painful to Santo's ears. He'd flown in from a meeting in Helsinki with Mads in his private jet and not bothered to stop at his hotel room first.

He felt...angry, disappointed. Frustrated and just damn tired of playing this game.

'She's not a game, Santo.'

'Then tell her the truth yourself and leave me out of it.'

'If you want to stop...'

'No.'

No. Santo didn't want to stop. He wouldn't break his promise to Pietro. The old man—who was *really* beginning to look every day of his sixty-two years—had made the visit out to Puglia especially.

They'd spent hours talking about it. About how Pietro had been reaching out to Analise Carson in secret. How he'd never stopped loving the woman he'd spent only a few short months with when she was travelling around Europe on her own.

Pietro had been devastated when she'd returned to England, believing that her family would never agree to let her be with someone like him, so he'd acted rashly and become engaged to a family friend from Naples. It hadn't taken long for the news to get back to Analise, who had found herself rebounding into the arms of Edward Carson. And when she'd discovered she was pregnant, it was too late. Edward had believed the child was his and proposed. It had all spun so out of her control that she'd been unable to stop it.

When Pietro had finally found out he'd broken the engagement amicably with his fiancée and tried to win Analise back, but they'd discovered just how dangerous Edward Carson could be. He might not have got his own hands dirty, but the 'mugging' which had broken Pietro's leg, collarbone and several ribs, as well as fracturing an eye socket had left him with all the money in his wallet. The message to Analise's 'ex' couldn't have been clearer. But that didn't stop Carson from going after Pietro financially for years. Every now and then Carson still poked and prodded, believing, like most, that Pietro's finances were simply the middle of the range business acquisitions that appeared on paper. But he hadn't been born the son of an ex-Mafia enforcer for nothing.

We just have to keep playing the long game, Santo.

The past and the present swam in his mind like flotsam, catching and snaring on thoughts and holding for a moment before slipping out of reach. Like mother, like daughter, Santo thought as he saw Eleanor talking to Kat and another member of the group that failed to draw any of his attention. He saw a glint and wondered whether it was fancy, or whether he'd seen the glitter of Eleanor's new engagement ring.

Someone passing gave him a strange look and he wondered whether the growl that had sat at the back of his throat had somehow drawn their gaze. It was possible. The control he usually had on his emotions was pushed to the limit this evening.

And he blamed it on her. Her and her absolute unwillingness to learn from her mistakes.

The announcement had been fairly quiet this time. Whether that was because of Edward's reluctance to acknowledge Eleanor any more or because of the insignificance of the man she had apparently *fallen in love* with, who could say.

Love.

Even the thought of the word turned his stomach and brought a sneer to his lips. He swallowed another mouthful of whisky and turned his back on her, telling himself that he didn't care what she did, as long as it kept her out of Edward's reach.

He spent some time catching up with Karl and Aditi, pleased to hear that Amita was getting on so well back in Jaipur at university. He could tell that Aditi missed her daughter, but they all agreed that she was better where she was. She'd found the gathering too intimidating last year, but her mother said she sent Santo her regards.

A little later he was cornered by Ivanov, who wanted to know when they could expect to see returns on the new expansion of the land in Puglia after the sale had gone through with Santo's neighbour. After that, Müller tried to get him to invest in his latest venture, and failed miserably.

All the while he sensed Eleanor on the outskirts of the crowd, being pushed closer and closer to where he stood, each footstep ratcheting up his pulse, pushing a little harder at the blood pounding through his veins. His irritation inching higher.

Unaccountably, he was absolutely convinced that she didn't want to be anywhere near him. And that, perversely, only pissed him off more. After their encounter last year, he'd thought, *hoped*, even, that she might have actually learned something. Might have grown up a little.

Her laugh, getting closer and closer, grated on already stretched nerves.

'How did he manage with Analise and Edward?' he heard someone ask.

'He...did well,' Eleanor replied, and Santo barely concealed his cough of disbelief. There wasn't even a chance that the hedge fund manager to whom she was presently engaged had even met Edward Carson. Not a single chance.

He could practically *feel* Eleanor bristling behind him.

'And how long until the wedding? Are you looking for a long engagement?'

'No, actually, we're hoping to marry in April.'

'So soon?'

'We're just so excited,' came the patently false reply from lips the flavour of which he could still taste on his tongue.

It was obscene. Her desperate plea for truth from him, and then *this*.

'Well, you and James have my congratulations,' insisted whoever it was Eleanor was speaking to.

Santo all but sneered, watching Eleanor smile and accept them graciously in the reflection of the large mirror on the opposite side of the wall.

Whoever it was made their excuses to leave, and he didn't have to turn around to hear the angrily delivered whisper from over his shoulder, aimed for his ears alone.

'Just stop it,' Eleanor bit out, glaring daggers at him in the mirror's image.

He clenched his jaw, intensely disliking that she thought she could have any say over his actions whatsoever. He glared back until she averted her gaze, smiling and waving at another guest.

Eleanor felt his gaze like a hand clasped loosely around her throat, a little like a leash with enough rope to run, but not get far. And that was the problem. It always had been. Her thoughts, her mind, her body's wants, always came back to him. Inescapably and inexorably. And she had realised this last year that if she had any hope of escaping this life, this world, she'd have to escape him too, wouldn't she?

He was just as much a part of this entire machinery as Edward Carson was. Even if he *did* want her in the same way that she wanted him—which she honestly didn't believe any more—there would always be *this*. There would always be one night a year spent amongst these people, the majority of whom made her skin crawl.

And even if there were times when she'd thought differently of him, when she'd thought she'd seen something else beneath the surface, she had been wrong, clearly. Because she'd seen the financials, read the reports in the newspapers, lauding the joint venture between the Sabatini Group and Ivanov Industries. Not to mention the supposedly secret project between Mads and Santo. No, the Italian was as deeply intertwined with this group of people as the rest of them. He might despise them as much as she did, but that wasn't stopping him from being here, year after year. And that was why she'd agreed when James had invited her for dinner early last year, believing that the only way to get over Santo was to meet someone else.

No, James didn't have the same dramatic impact that Santo had on her. Eleanor wasn't naïve, she knew it was highly unlikely that anyone would. She was bound to Santo by a connection forged at a moment in her life when she'd been so utterly impressionable. When he'd protected her, even as he'd teased her and taunted her. He'd changed her and she would be thankful for the rest of her life. But a part of her felt as if she was always missing the one piece of information that would make sense of their interactions, and a small part of her wondered whether *that* was the reason for her infatuation with Santo.

But it had been so different with James. He'd been... calm. Considered. Attentive. Kind. He wasn't trying to score points in some powerplay. And he had absolutely no interest in her family name or investments. He was handsome and nice and hadn't baulked when she'd intimated as much as she could about her family. She'd forced herself to tell him the truth—that theirs wasn't, and quite possibly never would be, a love match—and James had understood. What she wanted from their marriage was safety and security for her mother and brother, and freedom for herself. And, in exchange, what he wanted seemed almost easy to give: companionship.

In the meantime, Edward's chokehold on their interactions lessening just enough, she had been able to carve out some time with her mother, who had revealed her father's name to her. *Pietro.* That was all she knew. The way that her mother had looked when she'd spoken of him…it nearly broke Eleanor's heart. She knew in that moment that her mother had loved Pietro and had never stopped loving him.

She'd wanted to ask more, she'd wanted to ask if he'd tried to find them, if her father had tried to come for her, but she couldn't afford to ask that question. Couldn't afford to be so reliant upon another man ever again. And at least she knew with startling clarity she would never have that with James.

Eleanor found herself unable to avoid the reflection in the mirror. Santo was *still* looking at her. A flush of angry heat painted her cheeks and she went to walk away, when suddenly Dilly appeared right before her, forcing Eleanor back a step and causing her to brush up against the wall of Santo's immovable back.

'Congratulations,' Dilly said with disdain.

'Thank you,' Eleanor replied, trying to find her equilibrium.

'Maybe this time it will stick?'

Eleanor felt as if she'd been slapped.

'I mean, it would look almost incompetent to lose two fiancés.' Dilly leaned in, as if confiding, in the way that she used to when they were friends. Before Eleanor had caught her with Tony.

Eleanor felt indignation at Dilly's words swimming in her blood, rushing to her head, urging her to say or do something rash. She was so bloody tired of being everyone's punching bag. But next year would be different. Next year she would be married, and could finally stop coming to these damn things.

'I don't have to listen to this,' she said, trying to sidestep her one-time friend.

'What are you going to do? Run back to Daddy?'

Eleanor spun round on the woman, fury sparking like electricity. Dilly couldn't have known the effect of her words, would never understand how much they had cut and sliced and twisted. But this woman, who had been so wrong to do what she'd done, had no right to be angry with her when she had done nothing wrong. She'd never done anything wrong.

'I don't have to run back to Daddy,' Eleanor said in a low voice, with more control than she felt at that moment. 'I have everything I need right here. I have an audience of nearly two hundred of your nearest and dearest,' Eleanor continued with a smile on her face, while Dilly began to lose hers. 'I could easily tell them what I overheard you and Tony doing, but I haven't. If people know, it is because Tony told them, not me.' Eleanor took a breath and looked, really looked, at her once best friend. 'I know what desperation looks like,

Dilly,' she said not unkindly. 'And I can see it in you, coming out of every single pore.'

'You ruined me,' Dilly whisper-hissed in accusation.

'You ruined yourself,' Eleanor replied without missing a beat. 'So what are you going to do about it?'

'Do?' Dilly asked, as if genuinely confused.

'You got yourself into this mess. Stop blaming other people and do something about it.'

With that, Eleanor smiled, aware of the attention they had drawn, and placed a kiss on Dilly's cheek, hoping that she could wait until she'd left the room before wiping her mouth with the back of her hand.

Spinning on her heel, she exited the room, blind to the sea of faces swimming before her, driven forward by the building pressure in her chest. It was a sob, a cry, it was tears and oxygen, it was sadness, grief, loss wrapped in anger and frustration. But the one thing it wasn't was helplessness.

She just needed a moment to gather herself. Just one.

But then she felt him hot on her heels and her stomach flipped, her heart pulled on a string tied to him, yanked hard, and her body felt flushed for all the wrong reasons.

Oh, why wouldn't he just leave her alone?

She opened a door and slipped into the room, knowing that a closed door wouldn't keep him from coming after her. She backed into the room and was halfway across when Santo came in, closing the door behind him.

Battling hard against the realisation that she wasn't scared but thrilled, her breath punctuated the air between them. Why was he the man her body surrendered to? Why was he the man who made her pulse leap and her heart pound? Why was he the man who, no matter what she wanted, what she needed, she always came back to?

'I want you to leave,' she tried.

'No.'

'No?'

'No,' Santo repeated.

Every step he took into the room not only made her step back but also drew them closer and closer to that damn line that, once crossed, couldn't be taken back. But there was something primal in the air, working a magic that was unrecognisable to his brain, but known fully by his body.

It was the same alchemical reaction that always happened when they were near each other. As if they were magnets, unable to help the physics of their make-up. Drawn to each other, repelled from each other. It had worn him down to the last vestiges of his patience and it wouldn't take much for him to lose it altogether.

'You can't say no,' Eleanor accused, as if logic and etiquette had any place here.

'I just did,' he all but growled, hating that she had driven him to this, that he had become the very thing he'd never wanted to be. Completely driven by impulse and need. He clenched his teeth together, but one look at Eleanor and he could see that she was fighting this as much as he was.

'What is your problem?' she demanded.

'You, Princess. It's always you,' he said, closing the

gap between them as she came up against the back wall of the room.

Cristo, she was exquisite. He wanted her. It was that simple and that undeniable. And how much of a bastard did it make him that he didn't even care that she wore another man's ring?

He peered down at her, aware that he was using his body to crowd her, relishing the way that their need for each other filled what little air there was between them.

'Why are you angry with me?' she asked, staring up at him, wide-eyed and begging for something she probably didn't have the courage to name.

'I'm not angry, I'm *furious*,' he clarified.

Only that wasn't quite true, not any more. Because the fury that had ridden him so hard only minutes ago had been replaced and he had to call it what it was. Desire. Need. Wrapped in a fist so tight that no one could prise it apart.

No one but her.

She continued to stare up at him, as if aware that his arousal·had stolen the heat from his anger. Did she feel it too? The swollen throb that poured through his body with every beat of his heart whenever she was near, the fist that gripped his lungs and made it impossible to breathe.

'Why?'

'Because you demand honesty from me, yet everything about you is a lie,' he said, the truth slipping out into the air between them, surprising them both. Just the acknowledgement, just the memory of the promise she'd forced him to make, the lie she'd forced him to tell, tapped back into that heat and once again the magnets flipped and he was repelled from her, taking a few steps back, sucking air into his lungs that wasn't tainted with the scent of her body.

Merda, he needed to get control over himself. He should never have come in here. But when he turned he found her right back there in front of him, having crossed the room with silent steps. This was madness.

'You think this guy will be able to give you what you want?' he couldn't stop himself from demanding.

'Yes,' she said defiantly, her eyes flashing with warning.

'He'll be able to keep you, your mum and Freddie safe?' he scoffed, incredulous—incredulous and more than just a little outraged. From the background check he'd authorised, the man was inconsequential at best. He didn't have the power or the reach to protect her.

'Yes. Yes, he can.'

'So, you'll marry and then what?'

Eleanor shrugged as if confused by the question, the elegant line of her shoulders drawn with tension beneath the dusky pink silk dress she wore.

'Are you planning to hide out in suburbia for the rest of your life?' he demanded, pushing her again, stepping closer, daring her almost to run from him. *Cristo*, why was it that just the thought turned his blood to molten lava in his veins?

'If that's what it takes,' she replied, refusing to back down, refusing to bow to his blatant display of power.

'You won't last a week,' he sneered.

'I've lasted six already,' she bit back.

Santo clenched his jaw, his whole body on fire with the tension it took to hold himself back.

'Tell me he's what you want,' he growled.

'He's what I need.'

And while everything in his entire being roared at the thought that another man could be that for her, could fulfil that role for her, instead he latched onto the most important thing.

'Eleanor. You are a strong, capable woman who can get what she needs for herself. Tell me he's what you *want*.'

For a moment he saw it. The impact the first part of his sentence made on her. As if it were a surprise to her that someone would see her that way.

Did she not know? Did she not realise how amazing she was?

'You are capable of so much more than being a housewife,' he said. He knew that. He didn't even need to read Mads's updates to know that. Eleanor had become a highly valued member of his London office, having graduated with a first in her degree despite all the odds. She was wasting her potential and he couldn't stand it.

'There is nothing wrong with making a home,' she cried, her own anger painting her cheeks pink, the flashes in her eyes now exploding like fireworks.

'Of course not,' he wholeheartedly agreed. 'But you don't want that. You want more.'

She spun away from him in frustration, her fists clenched and her growl of frustration audible.

He felt some sympathy. After all, this was exactly how she made him feel.

'Why is it always like this?' she asked, still facing away from him.

'Haven't you figured that out yet, Princess?' he said before he could stop himself.

She turned, looking up at him, hoping for an answer. He would probably come to regret it, but he just couldn't fight it any more.

'It's foreplay,' he explained.

'Don't be ridiculous,' she dismissed, but the blush on her cheeks told him she knew.

'Some people like sweet nothings and pretty gifts. It appears you like something altogether different,' he said, as if observing the weather, while his mind already imagined a future where he could finally get his hands on her, when all this frustration and need was spent and he was free.

'I'm leaving,' she said.

'You can try,' he offered, having already seen how this would go down. It was inevitable really. Almost as if it were too late.

'What's that supposed to mean? I can leave if I want.'

'You can, but you don't want to,' he said, leaning forward, his lips just above her ear. 'This is the most fun you've had all year.'

'Don't be stupid,' she replied, staring ahead at his chest, but making no attempt to move away from the press of his body.

'Sorry, sweetheart. You made me promise not to lie to you,' he taunted, half cruel, half driven out of his mind with lust.

Her swift inhale pushed her chest against the neck-line, and pushed him even closer towards the precipice.

'Tell me you don't want this. Tell me I mean noth-ing to you. Tell me you haven't thought about this, like I have, every night for *years*.'

'I... I...' The word '*can't*' had barely left Eleanor's mouth when his lips crashed against hers.

The sudden shocking reality of what she had fanta-sised about for years stole her breath. He didn't wait, he wasn't patient, he just expected her to keep up—as if absolutely no time had passed between the kiss they'd shared two years before and now.

He walked them back to the far wall, her hands rais-ing of their own volition to grab the lapels of his dinner jacket, her fingers slipping on the silk before fastening more securely around the material and, before she knew it, *she* had taken the lead, *she* was the one pulling him into her, *she* was the one drawing them further back until they couldn't go any further.

Her back slammed against the wall at the same time as Santo's hand swept to the back of her head, cushion-ing any possible blow. But then, sneakily, he used that same movement to his advantage and angled her to him so that he could tease her lips open.

To compare this to their earlier kiss was almost laugh-able. Oh, God, she all but *dissolved* into him. The heady moment his tongue met hers was enough to stop time and steal a heartbeat. He was a thief, taking what she didn't know she wanted to offer. Her heart thundered in her chest, and all she could think was that it wasn't enough. That it would never be enough.

He trailed his fingers down the arch of her neck to her collarbone, while his other hand fastened her to him at the waist. As he held, she pulled, and she wanted more. Her hands flew to thread through his hair, to encourage him to take more, to show her more, to give her more.

Breathless, heated, heart racing and aching in places and ways that could never be appeased by any other man, pleading, begging words fell from her lips, incomprehensible wants, pressed into his kiss. Each one met by an answering growl of agreement, or encouragement, she couldn't tell any more.

His hand moved torturously along the side of her body, down her ribcage, skirting around the edge of her breast, sending a shiver of goosebumps across her skin, dropping to her backside, making her gasp, and finally to her thigh, where he reached for her leg. Hooking it over his hip, he pressed against her body powerfully, once, twice and the third time she could no longer deny what he was doing.

The mimicry of what she wanted more desperately than her next breath clogged her throat, thickened her blood and made her nearly blind with want. Again and again, she felt the press of his erection through the impossible barrier of their clothes, the large, hot, insistent ridge of his arousal *finally* proving beyond all reasonable doubt that he wanted her as much as she wanted him.

Her hands grasped his waist, not to stop him but to hold him, to delight in his need of her, to commit it to memory and to know what could have been. She teased herself with the feel of him, coming shockingly close to orgasm, which was enough to bring the sharp stab of sanity crashing down into her heart. She pulled back from the kiss, the breath panting in and out of her chest mixing with his hard inhalation and fast exhalation.

There was no touching moment like before, their foreheads pressed together, allowing the moment to sink in. No, instead, Santo glared at her, full of accusation, arousal, determination and resentment. In that moment she realised how truly he had proved his point. How James could never measure up to the wants and needs that Santo unleashed in her. Wants and needs deep within her, innate to her, part of her as much as her DNA.

She was devastated, he was victorious. But neither was happy.

He smoothed his shirt down over his torso, checked his belt and tugged on his cufflinks, all the while she was utterly incapable of speech.

He nodded to her once and then, with a, 'See you next year, Princess,' he left the room, the words less like a promise and so much more like a threat.

CHAPTER NINE

New Year's Eve last year, Venice

ELEANOR POSITIONED THE mask over her face, thankful that
this year's hosts, the Capparellis, had decided on a mas-
querade ball. After the bad press over her second broken engagement, all she'd wanted to do was hide. She'd
hoped that Edward would let her stay back at home in
England, but it appeared he still planned to use her as
bait to lure investors' attention with the hope of marrying her off to one of their sons.

Now twenty-six years old, Eleanor stood looking out
over the Venetian canal, lit with strings of white lights,
seeing couples being propelled along the night covered
waterway in gondolas, sharing romance and love, all
the things she began to fear that she might be now too
damaged to experience.

This time last year she'd honestly not thought that
she'd ever have to return to one of these events. She'd
thought she'd be married, her first year away from Edward, away from here and away from *him*. But she had
been so very wrong.

James had been almost alarmingly calm when she

had broken their engagement. Inside, she'd been torn to pieces, chewed up with guilt, knowing what she'd shared with Santo, seeing the perfect, easy future she'd envisioned slipping through her fingers.

But, once again, Santo had been right. And she hated him for it. Hated that he got to stand there and pass judgement over her actions, when they were so limited in the first place. But she'd used that anger, honed it and let it fuel her.

The one advantage of being at home, under Edward's control, meant she'd had no bills. And she was putting the money she'd earned from her job with Mads, especially after her recent promotion, to good use. After paying off the loan she'd taken out to pay the last year of her university fees, and to cover the few expenses she did have, she'd opened a savings account. And last year she'd started to turn her hand to investments. Some low yield, long-term, but some the opposite. And those were the ones that had paid off. Big time.

Freddie, now sixteen years old, picking up on the increasingly difficult emotional undercurrents wrecking their small family, had started to avoid coming home. She'd spent as much time with him as she could, telling him as much as she dared, which wasn't enough but was still something. Her brother could see that her hands were tied, but he was also frustrated and upset about being kept in the dark about something he knew but didn't actually understand.

Which meant that Eleanor had a lot of free time in the evenings to spend online on the stock market. She was good enough at picking through a company's financials to see a little more behind the scenes than most, and the knowledge that she had picked up from the world Edward had drawn her into had given her a strong basis for her investments. She had begun to build a rather impressive portfolio and relished the security that gave her. Because everywhere else it felt as if she was losing.

In the first years that had followed the shocking discovery of her parentage, survival instinct had made her focus on what was in front of her. But she had acclimatised to the way her life was now, and it wasn't enough just to accept things the way they were. The need for more was urgent in her blood.

Edward's attention had begun to wander, and she'd been able to speak to her mother more and more. Did her father even know about her? If he did, why hadn't he tried to reach her? In even some small way at least. The thought that he hadn't was painful, so much so that she'd tried to put it out of her mind.

Just like she had tried to put other things out of her mind, but Santo was always there, waiting for her every night as she closed her eyes.

'See you next year, Princess.'

Even now, a shiver rippled across her skin. He had known. Just like he always had. What was it about him that he saw so much? That he knew so much about her, if not more than she knew herself? She felt as if she'd lived with him inside her skin all year. Every thought was tainted by him, by what he would think, by what he would say.

Each imagined response whispered in her ear as he—in her mind—loomed from behind. Teasing, taunting, promising. But it wasn't just words. Her fantasies had run rampant. Each time the sensual anticipation of what they could share became more vivid, more lurid—just *more*. And no matter what release she tried to find for herself, it wasn't enough. It wasn't him.

She shook her head at herself in disgust. She had turned into an obsessive.

'Something bothering you this evening, Eleanor?'

It was so close to her daydreams that she half expected it to have been a figment of her imagination. But the heat of his body, the scent pressed against her senses, the way that she responded to the impact of his voice…those made it real. *He* was real. The thrill that went through her, as if he had pulled on the invisible chain that bound them together.

'How did you recognise me?' she asked, her hand reaching up to adjust the mask again.

'I'd know you anywhere, Princess.'

It had shocked him, as much as it would anyone, to discover that the first kiss that he had shared with Eleanor had not been an anomaly. Because the second kiss only confirmed what Santo had thought for some time—that, no matter how much he fought, denied and refused to believe it, Eleanor was the one and only woman for him. As such, he'd been left with no other choice.

After he had left her last year—only because had he not, he would have taken her right there, in a room with no lock on the door, when anyone could have walked in on them, and honestly, he probably wouldn't have even cared—he had confronted the fact that he would do whatever it took to make her his.

No doubts, no more second-guessing, no prevarication.

She had broken her engagement because he'd been right. Because she could never hide in suburbia, she could never hide behind a man. She deserved more than being safe, because she was strong enough to survive it. She deserved more than being secure, because the risk was worth the reward. And the rewards for her would be more than she could ever imagine.

And since then he had spent every waking minute of every day making sure that everything was in place, so that when he made his move *nothing* would stand in his way. He had successfully managed to disentangle his business from Edward Carson. Yes, it had meant reinvesting with some of the other families—committing to business relationships that he didn't want—just so that Carson would have no ability to impact the Sabatini Group, and thus, by extension, both himself and Eleanor, ever again.

And while she didn't know it *yet*, he would make one hundred percent sure that she never had to worry about her mother, her brother or Edward Carson ever again. The only thing playing on his mind was that Pietro didn't know. That he wasn't sure that Pietro would approve. He certainly wouldn't approve of what Santo had been wanting to do to the man's daughter for nearly as long as he'd known her. It was the first time he'd ever withheld something from the man who had been more like a father to him than his own, and it was a twist of the knife in his conscience. But Pietro would have to wait.

Santo spotted Eleanor at the edge of the crowd, something easing in his chest for the first time since he'd left her the year before. No more would he allow so much time to stand between them. Tonight he would see to that, he was determined.

He stalked towards her slowly, guests moving from his path as he closed the distance between them, anticipation and expectation burning in his chest and scouring his veins.

He came to stand behind her, taking a moment to inhale the sweet scent of her. To know that he would wake up with it in the morning nearly unmanned him right then and there.

'Something bothering you this evening, Eleanor?' he asked softly.

She started, the hitch of her shoulders enough to tell him that he'd caught her by surprise.

'How did you recognise me?' she asked, fiddling with her mask.

'I'd know you anywhere, Princess,' he told her truthfully. He could be blind, deaf, his tongue could have been ripped out, but he'd know this woman until his last breath. She was as much a part of him as the beat of his heart.

'Dance with me?' he asked, his palm upturned, open to her.

Eleanor's head turned half towards him, the profile of her face and the gold feather detail of her mask beautiful.

'Here?' she asked, her gaze locking onto his.

'No, out in the canal,' he teased and the edge in her eyes softened and warmed.

'Are you sure?' she asked, as if worried that he wouldn't want to be seen with her here, amongst these people.

He leaned forward, holding her gaze with his. 'Absolutely.'

A large space in the exquisite ballroom had been created for dancing—the orchestra, also masked, filled the hall with the sound of perfectly played waltzes. One piece was drawing to an end as Eleanor placed her hand in his and he led her to the centre of the room. It fitted so perfectly in his palm he almost forgot himself.

He noted a few whispers, felt more than a few gazes across the back of his neck, and hated the way that Eleanor stiffened at the feel of them too.

'Ignore them. You are the only one that matters here tonight,' he said as he led her to face him in a waist-hold. They stood, waiting for the music to start, and he marvelled at how right it felt to have her in his arms.

'What is it, *cara*?' he asked, noticing her gaze downward.

'I'm not used to pretty words from you,' she admitted with a smile.

Regret shot through him. They had lost so much time over the years, but no more. He would not, could not, let her go this time.

More and more couples filled the dance floor, but still they drew the most attention.

'I might find such things difficult,' he admitted. 'But

if you want them, you'll have them every single day,'
he vowed.

She looked up at him in surprise, a flush coming to
her cheeks, gold shards glittering in the deep brown of
her gaze. If this was her reaction to a few pretty words,
then he'd shower her with them every minute of the day.

Her gaze scoured his, as if searching his features for
the truth, hoping to divine his thoughts.

'What would you say?' she asked as the music began
and he swept them into a dance his mother had forced
him to learn when he'd been barely twelve years old.
And for the first time in his entire life, he was thankful
for the lesson. Because Eleanor moved like a swan on
a lake. Graceful, *beautiful*, poised, in all the ways that
made him feel like a clumsy oaf beside her.

'That you are the most precious thing in the world
to me,' he admitted. 'That my life doesn't make sense
when you are not here. That I ache to see you every moment of every day that I do not. That I want to know
what you think, how you think, why you think, so that
maybe, just maybe, I might understand you just a little
more. Because that has become my only worthy en-
deavour,' he said.

As they moved around the room and his words fell
in their wake, not once did she take her eyes from him.
The small smile that had curved her lips grew, millimetre by millimetre, until it was the most beautiful thing
he'd ever seen.

Titters from the crowd began to intrude and he didn't
want that. He wanted her all to himself, and he thought
that maybe this time she was ready to come with him.

Not because she was fleeing, or hiding, or drowning. But because she wanted to.

He drew to a halt, not caring or needing to wait any longer.

'Come with me?' he asked.

'Anywhere,' she replied, and for the first time ever in one of these horrible New Year's Eve events, Santo Sabatini felt joy.

Eleanor let him lead her away from the ballroom, down the stairs and out through doors, and she didn't care who saw them. As he led her out into the frigid winter's night air, she didn't feel the sudden sharp icy sting, she felt alive, her blood burning through her body, a heat that had nothing to do with temperature and everything to do with the slow burn that had taken her over the moment he'd whispered into her ear that night.

They slipped through the throng of tourists hoping to celebrate the New Year; blurred faces stared after the two beautifully dressed people in masks racing across the cobbled square. He drew her into the entrance of his hotel, his hand in hers all but dragging her over the threshold and up an exquisite wooden curved staircase, towards a door on the uppermost floor, only four storeys above the street level.

And all she could think was, *Now. Please, God, now.*

After all the times that things had got in their way, after mistakes and wrong choices, she suddenly feared so much that this too would slip through her fingers, so much so that she thought she felt tears press against the backs of her eyes.

His pace slowed as he drew her towards the door at the far end of the corridor. And this was it, she thought, panicked. He was going to change his mind, and her heart wrenched as if she had already lost him.

With his key card pressed against the scanner for the room, the door partially pressed open, Santo looked down at her, something like alarm passing across his features.

'What's wrong?' he asked, searching her eyes.

'I…' She bit her lip, worried about what she would say. 'I…' She shook her head and looked down.

He lifted her chin with his forefinger, forcing her eyes back to his.

'Please don't change your mind,' she whispered. She couldn't bear it if he turned her away now.

'Why would…' He trailed off, as if unable to finish the sentence, let alone the thought.

'Because you see me,' she whispered again. 'All of me, from the very beginning. You have seen *me*. Not Edward, not money, not access, not a prize. And now I want you to *know* me and…if you stop then I don't think that I could bear it.'

'Why would I stop?' he asked, confusion clouding his gaze.

'What if you don't like what you find? What if I'm not good enough for you?'

'*Cristo, amore mio*, that would never happen.'

'Even if I'm…' She could hardly bring herself to say it.

'Innocent?' he finished for her.

She clenched her teeth together and nodded, not

ashamed but embarrassed. Because she wanted him to
see her as a woman, not some silly naïve girl asking for
more than she could handle.

'Does that change things for you?' she dared to ask.

'Not at all, Eleanor. The only thing that will stop me
tonight is a word from you, *prometto cara.*'

His promise skated over her skin, leaving goosebumps in its wake. But all thought stopped the moment
that his lips met hers to seal the vow.

He kicked the door open with the back of his heel and
enticed her across the threshold with a kiss promising so
much that it filled her heart and soul. And she knew in
that moment that wherever he went, she would follow.

Her fingers reached up to wrap around his neck as,
at the same time, his hands reached for her, lifting her
from the floor effortlessly and into his hands. With one
hand supporting beneath her, the other cradled her head,
fisted in her hair, pulling just tightly enough to angle
her head where he wanted her, where he could plunge
his tongue into her mouth, where he could possess her
wholly, fully, *completely.*

In the second it took her to process the power of his
kiss she realised just how much he'd been holding back
before. Whether it had been decorum or the risk of discovery, it didn't matter because, released from his restraint, he was so far beyond her wildest imaginings.

Overwhelmed by all the sensations flooding her sys-
tem, her breath caught in her lungs and she forgot to
breathe. Her pulse leapt and dipped when he plunged
his tongue into her mouth, when he pulled her closer
into his body, when his hands swept around her dress,

as if trying to find a way beneath it to her skin, and she wanted that more than anything.

Holding her up above him, he walked further into the suite, not breaking the kiss until he put Eleanor down on the breakfast bar, where she was momentarily distracted by the most magnificent view. Not the nightscape across the Venice canals, but him. Staring at her as if he would never be able to tear himself away from her ever again.

He pushed at the thick skirts of her dress, closing his eyes as if in bliss when he finally found the sleek curve of her calf. Fascinated, she watched how young he suddenly appeared as he gently took her shoe in his hands, bending her leg a little between them so that he could dip his lips to the space just above, where her high heel was buckled.

It was perhaps the most erotic thing that had ever happened to her, her cheeks instantly flushing from the proximity of him, of his *mouth*, making her damp with want.

He looked up at her without bringing the kisses he pressed against her leg to an end, heat in his gaze, knowing...promise. He knew exactly what he was doing to her and he was watching her as intently as she was watching him, documenting each response, each reaction, the way that each touch thrilled, each kiss sent needles of sharp need into her lungs.

Panting now with desire for everything he could give her, her legs trembled beneath the weight of her want.

'I want to worship you,' Santo whispered honestly against her skin. 'I want you to know what that feels like.' And God, she wanted that too.

* * *

Santo wanted her to see what he saw. Her beauty, her strength, her power, her humour, her kindness and her confidence. He wanted her to know what he felt, but struggled to find the words that would make her understand how everything outside of them ceased to exist for him. Everything.

'I want you to feel nothing but pleasure,' he confessed.

Eleanor bit her lip as he trailed kisses up her calf, over her knee and across her thigh, the bare skin like silk. He wanted so much more for her than he'd ever had himself. He wanted to care for her throughout it, not steal it, bribe it or seduce it from her. He wanted her with him, in truth, in honesty and in pleasure.

'But if for one single minute you need me to stop, or to slow down—'

'Are you going to ask me for a safe word?' she said, trying to joke.

He stopped, his lips hovering barely an inch from her skin, and looked up at her, locking his gaze with hers. 'You are *always* safe with me.'

Her eyes glistened, emotion brimming to the edges, and he knew that she understood what he meant. That promise went beyond this night, to all the nights. To for ever, no matter what happened between them. It was unbreakable, written in the marrow in his bones. He would care for her, love her, until his last breath on this planet.

Barely able to contain his own feelings, he pressed another kiss and another against the flesh of her inner thigh.

Her sigh turned into a gasp that fisted his erection as

if she held him in the palm of her hand. Involuntarily, a growl escaped his lips and she shifted on the counter as if responses unfurled between them, back and forth on the tie that bound them together.

This was why it had always been inevitable. This was why she was the only woman for him now. Because his entire being depended on her, on what she felt, how she felt it, and how much better he could make it for her.

He gently parted her legs to make space for him fully, leaning forward to reach behind her to pull her closer to the edge, closer to him.

'I will stop if you want me to, but you have to tell me. So, I need you to talk to me.'

'You...you want me to talk to you?'

He leaned forward and kissed her, teasing her mouth open for him, one powerful thrust with his tongue against hers, before pulling back.

'I want you to tell me how it feels for you.'

He could see the flush on her cheeks deepen.

'What if I use the wrong words?' she asked, biting that lip of hers again.

'There are no wrong words here. There is nothing to fear, and nothing to be ashamed of, *cara*. I mean it,' he said, almost sternly.

Eleanor nodded, placing her trust in him, and he felt it like a gift. One that he was not worthy of in the least.

He kissed her again, swiftly, passionately, one hand pressing her into him, the other lifting her leg again behind her knee, over his hip, knowing that she could feel his need for her at the juncture of her thighs, knowing, as he ground against her, the moment he pressed against her clit because of the way her head fell back and the snap of pleasure rippled across her body.

He repeated the move again and she pressed, shaking, into him further.

'Words, *cara*,' he reminded her.

'Again,' she whispered.

'Why?' he asked, reaching the edge of his sanity.

'Because it feels good,' she said on panted breaths.

He slowly swept her skirt aside, lifting it over her knees, kissing each inch of flesh that was revealed across her thighs and higher, until finally he could see the dark, damp silk of her underwear, the musky scent of her driving him near feral with lust and want.

'May I?' he asked, with his thumb hooked into the waistband of her panties.

'Yes,' she said, her eyes so exquisitely full of desire, a strand of her hair falling loose as she nodded.

She raised her backside from the counter so that he could draw her underwear from beneath her and away from her body.

And then, with Eleanor open before him, the smile dropped from his mouth. Because she was incredible. Exquisite. She was it for him. There was no other option or possibility or future. It was all her.

There was nothing holding him back now. All he could do was let the fire consume them both. And that was the last thought he had as he bent his head to the juncture of her thighs and pressed open-mouthed kisses to her core, the taste of heaven he had fantasised about for years entering his bloodstream like a drug he would never quit.

* * *

Eleanor fell back against the wall, her hands fisting the edge of the table, knuckles white, trying to hold on, while Santo thrust her into a pleasure so acute she thought she'd break apart if she took another breath.

Curses filled her mouth and she thought, impossibly, that she could tell Santo was smiling as he pressed yet another open-mouthed kiss against her. His hands pressed her thighs open to him, his thumbs massaging gentle circles as his tongue laved over her clit in lazy sweeps that sent shivers across her entire body.

Oxygen battled against pleasure in her lungs and if she could survive on bliss alone she would happily do so, but couldn't, so gasped for breath as he pushed her closer and closer to the edge.

She writhed against him and he growled against her delicate flesh, nearly splitting her apart with desire. He did it again, and she cried out from the sensation alone. He circled his finger around her entrance, the feeling exquisitely new, teasing, making her want him there more than she could have possibly imagined.

'Cara?'

'Yes, please. Please, Santo…'

The words tripped over themselves as they fell from her lips. She would beg if she had to, but he would never let her do that because he was already where she needed him and then he thrust into her with clever, knowing fingers that filled her, the palm of his hand pressing against the rest of her as his tongue teased her clitoris to the point of near madness.

'Oh, God,' she hissed out. 'Santo, I…'

'Breathe,' he whispered. 'Breathe into it, let it fill you,' he guided. 'Let yourself come.'

He didn't push her further than what she could handle but instead deepened her experience for her, letting it sweep at her feet like the tide rather than a tsunami, letting her sink into it rather than drown, as if it were something to luxuriate in.

Breath after breath, swallowing down pleasure in a way she'd never known, never experienced, as her orgasm built from the ground up, from where he pressed his tongue to her, from where he added a second finger to fill her, from where he held her so securely against him. Her orgasm was like Santo himself, slow, inexorable; it stalked her like prey, closing in on her with a fatefulness that she couldn't escape, that she didn't want to escape.

He whispered words of encouragement against her, unintelligible to her overstimulated mind, but known instinctively by her body. She unfurled for him, she opened to him, wanting more, like an insatiable being hunting her own pleasure even as it stalked her, until finally her body couldn't take it any more.

With one final sweep of his tongue she exploded like the fireworks filling the night sky.

CHAPTER TEN

New Year's Eve last year, Venice

IN HER MIND she was distantly aware that Santo had gathered her into his arms and gently pulled her from the countertop, carrying her over to the large, soft leather sofa that looked out at the Venetian night sky, where stars vied with fireworks above waterways that reflected it all over again on shifting silken waves.

He lay back against the head of the sofa, pulling her onto him, keeping her in his arms.

'Did we miss New Year?' she asked when she found her voice again. He shook his head, his lips resting against the top of her head, ruffling her hair a little, and she didn't mind it a single bit. 'We've never done that.'

'*That?* No, I'd most definitely remember if we'd done that before,' he insisted.

'No,' she said, laughing and slapping the hand that was secured around her waist as if he never wanted to let her go. 'Seen the New Year in together.'

They'd either been with other people or they'd been pulled apart by other people. Even this moment felt stolen. As if, at some point, reality would come crashing down to take it away from her, just like everything else she'd thought she'd had in her life.

Eleanor turned her head to burrow against his chest as if he could ward off her fears. Her hand slipped beneath his shirt, where it had come open at his neck, and relished the hot skin, the texture of the swirls of hair that dusted his chest. And just like that, her curiosity was ignited, desire curling up like a flame from the ashes. She twisted in his lap, unbuttoning his shirt with curious fingers, before his hand came down around them.

'Cara,' he said, shaking his head, 'we can stop here. We can take it as slow as you want or need.'

But they couldn't. She didn't know what it was, waiting there on the horizon, she didn't know how it would happen, but she felt that this was it for them. That they *didn't* have all the time in the world. Whether it was because of the past or because of how it always was between her and Santo, something would happen to take this from her, and she wouldn't waste a single moment she had with him.

'This is what I want, Santo,' she said and meant it truly. 'You. I want you so much that I...' She stopped herself, but saw the questions in his eyes. 'I can't explain it...words don't explain it...' She shrugged. So she crawled up to take his lips in hers and poured every inexplicable, complicated, messy, passionate, desperate feeling she had for him into her kiss.

She wound her fingers into his hair and rose onto her knees, straddling his hips, before pressing herself down into his lap. He lurched forward to meet her, feeding off her passion, increasing it, multiplying it exponentially, his arms around her waist, holding her in the way that only he ever had, as if she were both incredibly precious and strong enough to take it—to take *him*.

This was what had been missing from her life, this was who she could love with unrestrained abandon, not without fear, and not without caution, but *with* those things, making it so much greater than anything she could have imagined. And it scared her witless.

He shifted her around him and she felt the hard length of him beneath her and she let the sensations draw her back into the sensual bliss he offered her.

His hands were full of her and it would still never be enough. Stomach muscles taut, he held himself and her upright as she pulled at the buttons on his shirt, shucking it from his shoulders, her palms smoothing over his skin as if learning the feel of it.

Cristo, her skin was like silk. Her tongue tangled with his as his hands swept across her body to find the fastening that held the dress together. As if sensing his impatience, she smiled against his lips and guided his hands to the buttons at her back, to tiny buttons that, when undone, unwrapped the dress like a present.

Before she could be revealed, his hands slipped beneath the gold layers of stiff silk and tugged the material from her body. And there she was, naked, and he nearly lost his mind.

Was this how it would be—that she would push him to the edge of his sanity? Was it something that someone like him could risk?

Her gaze beckoned him back to her, but a part of him

edged away, inch by inch, seeking a self-protection that was never coming back. He was done for—a lost cause.

But that didn't mean he should stop protecting her.

'Santo?'

Like a siren song, she called and he went to her as if she were his redemption rather than his damnation. He rocked beneath her and relished the shiver that ran up her body. Thrusting upward as she pressed down against him, goosebumps broke over his skin as she moaned in pleasure.

Unable to wait any longer, Eleanor's hands went to the fastening of his trousers, slipping the eye from the hook and releasing the zip. He couldn't take his eyes off her as she studied him, slowly pulling him free from his briefs, her hands around his length enough to make him come like some untried youth. He barely repressed the growl forming in the back of his throat but, from the knowing smile pulling at her lips, she'd heard him anyway. And liked it.

She looked up at him, the humour passing from her eyes. 'I don't want anything between us,' she said solemnly as she stroked the length of him again.

He bit his lip, trying not to be seduced by her desire.

'You should always use protection, *cara*,' he warned, aware of the irony of him lecturing her on protection when the thought of her being with anyone but him was untenable. 'For health, for contraception,' he bit out through the waves of pleasure her inexperienced hands teased from him. He was barely holding on and she was offering him everything he could ever want, whilst risking his worst nightmare—the continuation of his line. Of his genes. Of his *father's*.

He held his forehead against hers and tried to keep himself from thrusting into her caress.

'I'm on contraception.'

Her words pressed against his lips, and this time he was unable to hold back the groan that she swallowed as she opened her mouth to his in a kiss.

This woman was his undoing.

And then he cursed for a different reason.

'Bedroom,' he said against her mouth.

'No time,' Eleanor replied, pulling his waist between her legs.

'We will *make* time,' he commanded as he stepped back, plucked her from the sofa, hauled her into his arms, smiled when she squeaked, and stalked towards the bedroom. He was damned if he'd let her first time be some desperate scramble on a sofa.

He carried her down the corridor, almost disbelieving that he had her in his arms. That this time was theirs, finally. He toed the bedroom door open and, in the gentle upward lighting, made his way to place her gently on the bed.

She was utterly beautiful to him. It was a rush of knowledge, of blood, of conviction, of want, and he wasn't ashamed that he shook from the power of it. In that moment, he nearly turned back. He wasn't worthy of her, of this. There were things that Eleanor didn't know. But, just as his conscience began to stir, she sat forward, a frown between her eyes, a thread of concern that he never wanted to see passing across her exquisite features, and in his rush to reassure her, his thoughts fled.

He kneeled on the edge of the bed, coming for her, relishing the delight that now filled her gaze.

'You're wearing too many clothes,' she accused, as if in a sulk.

He cocked his head to the side, testing the game she wanted to play.

'What are you going to do about it, Princess?'

She rose to her knees, meeting him much closer on the bed than he'd expected. His entire body reacted, the hairs on his skin raising, the tightening of his muscles, ready for action, bound by restraint. A little smirk pulled at her lips and it was almost adorable. But the humour dropped beneath sharp need, when her hands went to the waistband of his trousers and pushed the material from his hips.

His jaw ached with the tension running through his body, holding him back, letting her explore as she wanted to. He pulled back enough to remove the loose trousers from his legs, to find her frowning at his briefs.

'Those too,' she commanded imperiously.

And he barked out a laugh. 'As you wish,' he said, his thumbs hooking into the band and drawing them slowly from his legs, delighting in Eleanor's fascination.

Her sharp inhale when she saw all of him pulled him back to her innocence, to why he hadn't just taken her up against the wall, as he'd wanted, the moment they'd crossed the threshold.

He was about to reassure her, remind her that they didn't have to do *anything* she didn't want, when she came to the edge of the bed, still on her knees, her cool little hands pressing into his body, his skin, his torso, around his hips and finally, exquisitely, around the length of him.

His head fell back as she explored him, as she felt her way around him, learning while she mystified him. But when he felt her mouth close around him, he nearly yelled out loud. He wanted to tell her she didn't have to, but he was drowning in a sea of such pure bliss it was near pain.

'Eleanor…' Her name was a plea and a prayer on his lips. *'Cristo.'*

Her response was a moan of delight around the hard length of him. Her tongue, the wet heat, the vibration of her pleasure was too much, and with a resolution that took more strength than he liked, he gently drew her away from him and pulled her up to face him.

'Did I do something wrong?' she asked, eyes wide, worried.

'Absolutely not,' he managed through the pounding in his chest. 'But if you want me capable of anything more we have to stop there. For now,' he said, more to reassure her than expecting more.

Realisation dawned in her gaze, a slight flush rose on her cheeks, and in that moment he thought that the crack in his heart began to close just a little. He kissed her then, covering the little fissures shifting like tectonic plates in his soul. He kissed her gently back against the bed, her arms sweeping up around his head, enfolding him, protecting their kiss against the outside world. He kissed the inside of her upper arm and just relished the heat of her body, the scent of her driving him wild. She opened for him, her legs gently wrapping around him, unconsciously guiding him to where they both wanted to be.

'Remember, *cara*, talk to me. Tell me what you feel, what makes you feel good, what doesn't, when you want me to stop,' he said in between kisses.

'If. *If* I want you to stop,' she insisted.

He smiled, but the seriousness remained in his gaze. 'It might hurt.'

She nodded, understanding and expectation serious in her eyes as he nudged himself at her entrance. The slick wet heat of her was urging him on, but he controlled himself with a ruthlessness that bordered on pain. Slowly, he leaned into her, inch by inch, filling her, joining with her, hating that the pure ecstasy of it for him caused her pain, the price she was paying indecent in that light. And in that moment he knew that nothing would ever be the same again.

The feeling of intrusion was almost overwhelming.

'Breathe, *cara*.'

Eleanor did as he asked, relaxing her body into it. Slowly, just like before, pleasure emerged from the pain, breath by breath, inch by inch, and her body, as if it knew him, as if it recognised him, began to unfurl for him.

As she adjusted to the size of him, she began to feel other things—the satisfaction of him inside her, the sense of completeness that began to fill her. The more she wanted him, the deeper she wanted him. The way that when he moved, he pressed against the bundle of nerves that snapped intense pleasure through her body.

A gasp fell from her lips and Santo responded by moving exactly the same way again.

'Good?'

'Amazing,' she hissed on an exhale.

'In what way?' he asked, and she could tell that he was struggling. Struggling to hold himself back, struggling to care for her, to protect this for her. To make it special for her.

'I never knew it could feel this way,' she admitted as he slowly filled her again, her head falling back on the pillow, her body rising to meet his. 'As if I had been empty until now,' she said as he drew back, the slide so delicious, and once again the gentle tide of her orgasm began to build. 'As if I had always missed you and never known it.'

He pushed into her slowly, deeply, as if he *was* that tide, gently covering her with a pleasure that was as strong as a life force. Not terrifying, not plunging towards the edge of a cliff, but, once again, accepting that inevitable conclusion where he would join her as they willingly stepped into the abyss together.

She started to shiver under the weight of that pleasure.

'*Cara?*'

'It's so much, what you do to me. It's everything,' she said in wonder as she breathed through a bigger wave of pleasure, as if they were wading into deeper and deeper waters.

Santo's head dropped to her chest, her hands coming to wrap around him, holding him to her breast as he teased her nipples. His movements became less smooth, and she knew that he was as affected as she was. His skin, slick with the same sweat as her own, the gentle slap of his body against hers, the gasps and moans no longer distinguishable between them as they came closer and closer towards this inescapable and undefinable *thing*.

Eleanor lost her breath, lost her sense of self, only knowing him, only knowing this. Her orgasm swept over her, over Santo, drawing him with her as they fell together...always together.

Eleanor woke, realising that the bed was empty. Smoothing circles on the cool sheets where Santo had been, she shook away the heavy sleep she had fallen into and sat up in the bed. Frowning, she pulled the silk throw from the bed and, wrapping it around her, she went in search of him.

He wasn't in the en suite bathroom, so she passed through the open bedroom door and, barefoot, made her way back towards the main part of the suite.

'No, it's not like that,' Santo insisted, his voice low.

Eleanor hung back at the threshold of the sitting room, reluctant to intrude on something that was clearly deeply personal. Santo was on the phone, wearing nothing but his black trousers. For a moment, she allowed herself to indulge in the planes of his muscled torso, remembering the feel of his skin against her palm, her lips... and deep within her. She cast her gaze back to where he'd placed her on the countertop, a fierce blush rising to her cheeks, purely from the memory of the pleasure he'd brought her there.

'No, absolutely not,' Santo whisper-hissed again, drawing her attention back to him, his hand slashing through the air like punctuation.

Frowning, curiosity drew her a step forward into the room when his next words stopped her dead.

'She might be your daughter, Pietro, but you sent *me* to look after her,' he bit out angrily.

Pietro.

The name sounded like a bell in her mind, casting ripples across her thoughts, her memories... Pietro. The name of the man who was her father, her mother had confided. The father who she had put from her mind because he hadn't come for her. Because he hadn't wanted her.

'I don't care what you think, I'm going to—'

Eleanor's head snapped up as Santo's words cut off, to see him staring at her reflection in the window.

'I have to go,' Santo said, ending the call without taking his eyes off her.

Neither moved for what felt like an eternity. And then they both moved at once, Eleanor away from him and Santo towards her.

Nausea hit her so hard, so fast, she was nearly sick.

Pietro.

He knew her father.

He had lied to her.

He had *been* lying to her the whole time.

'You sent me to look after her.'

'What's going on?' she asked with numb lips, as a stranger stared back at her from the other side of the room.

'Eleanor, I...' Santo's mouth shut, opened and shut again.

Start, stop, start, stop—it had always been like that for them. So much so it made her dizzy.

'You know my...my father,' she said, her voice breaking on the last word.

'Yes.'

Her head swam and the sands shifted beneath her feet all over again.

'You *knew* he was my father the whole time,' she stated, trying to pull all the threads together.

'Yes,' Santo confirmed, the words like bullets getting closer and closer to their mark.

Her hand pressed against her lips to stop the shock from overwhelming her. From escaping. From betraying her. He knew her father, he'd known. He'd known when...

'I asked you not to lie to me,' she said, remembering that night, remembering the desperate need she'd felt then, and now, never to experience this kind of truly life-altering devastation. Her breath shuddered in her lungs.

'Eleanor, it's not what you think,' Santo said, a plea in his gaze as he approached her.

She threw up a hand to ward him off.

The buzzing that she heard in her ears grew louder and louder. 'You promised. You *promised* you wouldn't lie to me.'

Something happened to him then. She saw it distantly through the haze that was slowly wrapping itself around her.

'Yes, I did,' he said, pulling himself to his full height. As if he were shedding the person that she had known only moments ago, the person she had given herself to. 'I did, because I made a promise long before the one I made to you, and I believe that those two promises weren't mutually exclusive.'

'Mutually exclusive?' she just about managed to repeat. 'This is my *life*, Santo.'

'And it is mine. I owe a debt to your father.'

A knee-jerk reaction had her thinking of Edward, instead of the name of the man who Santo knew more than she did. Enough to make a promise, enough to pay a debt.

She shook her head as he made another step towards her.

'I meant everything that we shared tonight, Eleanor. Everything I said, everything I did.'

'You lied to me,' she cried, the outburst shocking them both. 'You lied to me, and that's not even the worst of it. Because what *is*, Santo, is that you knew *then*, when you made that promise, what it would do to me if I found out. You made that promise, knowing what breaking it would do to me.'

The betrayal was devastating. Her heart tore apart as she reimagined the last eight years under a new lens. One from Santo's perspective, of knowing more about her than she knew about her own life. Each successive New Year's Eve overlaying the next, seeing things

differently, remembering little oddities—a vague rec-
ollection of Santo talking to her mother. Of Edward in-
terrupting her and Santo.

'Does my mother know? That you know my father?'

The muscle in his jaw flexed. 'Yes.'

'Does Edward?'

'I think he may have suspected,' Santo admitted.

'What else did you lie to me about?'

Something flickered in his gaze. Not a lie as such,
she was beginning to see, but something else. 'How else
have you interfered with my life?' she demanded, thinking through all the possibilities. She came to the realisation almost as he opened his mouth to speak.

'I spoke to Mads before you...'

Eleanor's legs nearly gave way, the hand she thrust
out to the wall the only thing keeping her up.

Her job. The one thing she'd had. The *one* thing she'd
thought she'd achieved herself. And everything that had
followed from that job, fruit of the poisoned tree. Lies.

Everything.

Could she even trust him? Could she trust anyone in
her life? Every single person had lied to her, kept secrets from her. Everyone.

'I need you to leave,' she whispered, wrapping the last
thread of determination she had left around her heart
like a bandage. She didn't care that it was his hotel room.
He could wait out in the hall naked for all she cared. But
she needed to gather her things, *herself*, and she couldn't
stand him watching her while she did.

'No, Eleanor. I'm not leaving until we talk this out.'

'There is nothing to talk about,' she spat.

* * *

Santo wrestled with control, anger, frustration, fear. She was slipping through his fingers, he could feel it, and it terrified him. But fear had never been a friend to him and it wasn't going to start now.

'Of course there is—this is worth fighting for, Eleanor.'

'Fighting for? Worth it?' she demanded, glaring at him from where she stood. 'You ruined this before it even had a chance, Santo. You knew what lying to me would do.'

'They were lies to keep you safe, Eleanor,' he ground out, frustration and fear pushing him to a point he knew was wrong. Pushing him into a corner that he knew he'd fight his way out of.

'Lying to yourself now? That must be a new experience for you,' she threw at him.

'Oh, don't be such a child, Eleanor. Things aren't so black and white,' he lashed out.

Fury whipped into her gaze. 'You don't get to accuse me of being a child, while saying all this was to protect me,' she bit back. 'You don't think that keeping these secrets has cost you too—kept you isolated, separate from forming proper relationships based on trust, on understanding?'

'Secrets have kept the people I love safe,' he growled, closing the distance between them, anger making them both rash.

'Now who's being the child?' she accused. 'Secrets kept me from making a choice, of doing things by myself, without you, without being dependent on you, on

my mother, on whoever my father is. Secrets are just a
way of manipulating people when you can't, or won't,
trust the decisions they will make on their own. It's *your*
way of manipulating people because you don't trust anyone enough to let them in.'

Injustice tore through him that she would so wil-
fully refuse to see what he did for her, what it cost him
to do for her.

'Me not letting anyone in? Me not trusting enough?'
he demanded, his hurt running away with him. 'You
wanted me to know you, all of you,' he said, using her
words against her. 'But you don't want to know me. *All*
of me. Once again, you're going to run away the very
first chance you get. What is it going to take for you
to stand your ground and fight for what you want, Eleanor? Because, apparently, it's damn well not me,' he
finished, his words a devastating crack in the already
fragile bond between them.

'You have *never* shown me all of you!' she cried out,
the tears in her eyes dissolving his resolve like acid
rain. 'Whether you're lying to me or lying to yourself,
the man I thought...' she clamped her lips together and
he could see her struggle to find a word that wouldn't
betray them both '...the man I thought you were was a
fabrication. You know everything about me, every single
secret I have, but I only know what you let me know. I
would have stood my ground for you if you had been
willing to show me who you truly are,' she finished on
a whisper, defeated.

He shook his head, her confession slipping through
the cracks of his hurt, and leaving only what he had ex-

pected to see, what he needed to see. She didn't want *him*. He wasn't enough. For her. For his mother. He'd never been enough. His heart broke under the weight of her words.

'I don't believe you. You, me, this—' he gestured between them '—it was nothing more than a distraction for you. It was you wanting to play with a boy who Daddy didn't approve of. Because, deep down, Eleanor, no matter what happened between you, you're still that same little girl looking for Edward Carson's approval and I would certainly never meet that.'

'How can you say that?' she demanded, her cheeks suddenly pale, her deep brown eyes wounded.

'Because you're still there!' he yelled. 'You're still playing by his rules, you're still bowing to his commands.'

'He has my family,' she bit back.

'Your mother is an adult, and your brother is barely a year away from being one. They can make their own decisions, so why haven't you?' he demanded. 'Maybe you should ask yourself that as you sit in your ivory tower where you look down upon us mere mortals and cast your judgement,' he growled.

Cristo.

He shook his head, the crack in his heart widening with every beat. He had to get out of here. Distant thuds exploded beyond the window as the crowds in the Venetian streets shouted their countdown to midnight.

Ten, nine, eight...

He grabbed his keys, his phone and his shirt from the back of the sofa.

Seven, six, five...

The horrible words they'd hurled at each other echoed in his mind as he made his way to the door.

Four, three, two...

And as the silence rained down, more deafening than any explosion, he pulled the door to the suite open and didn't look back as he left.

One.

CHAPTER ELEVEN

New Year's Eve tonight, Brussels

ELEANOR CARSON APPROACHED the stone steps towards the gothic building that housed this evening's New Year's Eve party knowing that, one way or another, it would be the last time she would ever come to one of these events. And she was more than ready for that to happen.

It had been three hundred and sixty-five days since she'd last seen Santo Sabatini. Yet, despite that, she'd thought of him almost every single minute of every single day. She had been a wreck after last year. She had thought of him as her anchor, the North Star by which she navigated her life, her route through the madness of this place and these people.

But discovering that he'd lied, knowingly, willingly and continually, for their entire relationship had coloured everything. Every interaction, every exchange, look, word. All that time he had known who her real father was. And yes, she'd been devastated that he'd kept that from her, but what had been worse was that he'd kept *himself* from her.

Eleanor didn't like looking back at those first few

weeks. She could barely remember them, but what she could recall wasn't pretty. She'd felt utterly empty, with nothing to numb the bone-deep ache that had settled beneath her skin and taken up residence.

Her mother had tried and cajoled but, being part of the chaos Eleanor was trying to find her way through, was unable to help. Freddie had wanted to delay his return to boarding school, but Edward refused to allow it. But her brother had sneaked back three days later, when Edward was away. At seventeen, bright blue eyes and blond hair, huge tears rolling down his cheeks, he'd begged and pleaded with her to tell him what was going on.

In that moment she'd realised that she was doing exactly what she had accused Santo of doing. She was keeping secrets from her brother in the hope that it would protect him from the fallout. From Edward. And, deep down, she was forced to face the fact that Santo had been right about that too. That what she had been *really* afraid of, why she hadn't left or fought back against Edward, was the terrifying thought that her brother and her mother would let her be exiled. That they would choose Edward over her. And that she would be left alone. Truly alone in this world.

She and Freddie had spent two days talking and crying and planning. Freddie had been so angry and hurt about the secrets they'd kept, and as she'd explained how terrified she'd been of losing him she'd begun to wonder if that was why Santo hadn't told her the truth, her mother too.

She'd returned Freddie to the boarding school and made up an excuse that wouldn't get back to Edward.

In the Easter holidays Freddie had convinced Edward to let the two of them go to 'Europe', Edward naively believing that he had enough control over her to stop her from doing something 'stupid'.

Which was how it had come to pass that Freddie had accompanied her to meet her father, Pietro Moretti, in the late spring. It had been one of the scariest things she'd ever done, but that Freddie was with her meant the absolute world. She knew then that, no matter what happened, what Edward did or threatened, she would never be alone. She was loved and she loved. Greatly. And that was far more important than blood ties and truths.

Pietro Moretti was older than she'd imagined—that or time hadn't been kind. The poor man had been as nervous as she was, but beneath the cream awning of a café in Rome, conversation unfurled in a way that swept away hesitancy and heralded a tide of familiarity that struck her bone-deep. She hadn't expected it, but it was there. They shared mannerisms that were impossible but undeniable, and regrets that would never be healed but could be soothed.

She could tell that Pietro had been sad that Analise wasn't there with them, but it had been important to Eleanor for this to be just for herself. Analise had understood, and that was enough. Eleanor's feelings towards both her parents were complex. She couldn't deny that there was a deep sadness that her father hadn't been able to come for her and her mother hadn't been able to be truthful with her, but she could also recognise that, had they been different, she wouldn't have had Freddie in her life, and she wouldn't trade him for the world.

Eleanor walked up the red carpet covered steps, wondering how many of the guests would have noticed the slight fraying at the edge, or the smears of mud and wet gathered from rain-covered streets. Not many, she decided as she presented her invitation. Now the scales had fallen from her eyes, Eleanor could see the darkness that touched everything about these people and these events, because no amount of money could hide the gluttony, selfishness and greed that were at the heart of nearly everyone here.

She hadn't talked about Santo with Pietro. It had been too much of a sore subject for her to broach. But he had tried. Just before she'd left him that afternoon in Rome, he had told her how good a man Santo was. Tears had filled both their gazes and she'd left with a twist in her heart.

Freddie had flown back to London, but she'd decided to stay on in Italy for a while, seeing some of her father's country. It was hard to distinguish the hope for connection with her birthright and the feel of the country as a stranger, but she'd found her way down south to Puglia almost by accident. And once she had ensured that Santo was away in London on business, she couldn't stop herself from heading out to the olive groves where the owner of the Sabatini Group had his residence.

There had only been a few people on the public tour at the unseasonable time of year and the estate manager had proudly shown off the grand estate. Rows and rows of olive trees filled the groves, some only just planted and others established over years. There was something incredibly beautiful about the vegetation blooming beneath the spring sunshine.

The tour had passed by a villa that looked so homely and inviting she had nearly refused to believe it when the manager had told them proudly that it belonged to the owner of the Sabatini Group.

The manager had explained how Signor Sabatini spent as much time amongst the olive groves as his staff, caring for the land far beyond what was expected for such a busy man. And it was evident, not just in the health of the land, but the happiness of his staff. And she'd realised then that the things Santo chose to keep secret, the things he kept to himself, was what he valued the most, so much that he couldn't risk any of the families seeing that and using it against him.

It was like seeing him for the first time, she'd felt, as if she'd seen him, untainted by vows and heated exchanges, untainted by *them*. Here, she could see the real Santo, in the soil, the work, the place that he had carved for himself in the world, and she liked that man, was impressed by him.

And it had given her hope. Hope that had led her all the way here tonight. To *him*.

Two suited men held the doors open for her to pass through and she entered the Black and White formal ball planned for that evening by the Fouriers. As she walked into the large ornate gothic hall, decorated in gold and cream on one side, and black and silver on the other, she squared her shoulders, a wry smile gently pulling at her lips at the gasps and whispers as she passed.

The crimson silk dress hugged every inch of her figure, and matched the slash of carnal red lipstick she wore on her lips. It was a silent battle cry, and she intended full well to wage war tonight.

She was done playing their games and by their rules.

With his back to the large entrance on the other side of the hall, Santo heard the ripple of consternation shiver out across the guests.

Only one woman could do that.

Eleanor.

He'd honestly thought that she wouldn't come tonight. He knew that she'd met with Pietro earlier in the year, had tried to ignore the rumours and gossip about what she was up to. He'd told Mads that he no longer wanted to know about what she was doing and how she was getting on, but he'd been like an addict, desperate for a fix, and his only solution had been to cut himself off from her completely.

For months following their night together he'd been utterly unbearable. To have gone from such incredible highs to such incredible lows in the space of what had felt like minutes had been utterly devastating. But the accuracy of Eleanor's accusations that night had been inescapable.

The dramatic contrast between what he'd thought they'd have together, the future he had constructed in his mind, and what she had shown him he had in fact offered her, had left him numb to almost everything around him. He'd let things go at the Sabatini Group, his panicked assistant and board desperately scrabbling to cover in his absence.

He'd blocked Pietro's calls and ignored his mother as he'd cut himself off from everyone and everything. And eventually he'd found himself at his father's grave for the first time since he'd been put in the ground.

He'd thought about bringing a bottle of whisky for the bastard who had shaped Santo's life with fists and fury, and then decided that he wasn't even worth it. For days he'd come back again and again, pacing and cursing him to hell and back and hating that what Eleanor had said was true; it *had* been safe for him to hide behind the lie. He'd made that promise knowing as much and, coward that he was, he had hidden from the truth the last time they'd been together.

Because if he could get away with showing her only what he wanted her to see, if he could cast himself in the role of her protector, he might just be able to make up for what he had never been able to do for his mother.

And by the time his mother came to find him at Gallo's graveside, he'd realised that he would never have been able to use Eleanor to appease the hurt in his heart. Not while he was still lying to her and himself. And there, by his father's grave, in his mother's arms, he'd wept like the child he'd never been allowed to be. For the fears he'd never been allowed to express and the love he'd so desperately wanted, no matter how much he'd denied it.

Santo braced against the memory of it, forcing himself not to tense against it, not to push it away, but to welcome it in, to let it wash over him and accept his feelings about it. It was a hard thing to do, given that he'd spent so many years refusing to even acknowledge such a thing.

Mads and Kat glanced between him and over his shoulder, and the sympathy and concern that he saw in their gazes told him that she was getting closer. The fact that they were worried about him was enough to let him know just how awful he'd been since the last time he'd seen her.

Mads had been the first person Santo had turned to when he'd come away from his father's grave. He just hadn't realised, truly realised, how isolated he had kept himself, until Eleanor had accused him of it. How much he'd done that to *protect* himself. And the stark irony of discovering that he hadn't been protecting Eleanor but actually only protecting himself this entire time had nearly brought him to his knees.

So he had started with Mads, letting him in, bit by bit. And Mads had paid that back in kind, slowly opening up to Santo, enabling them to form a friendship that Santo knew would last, no matter what. He had also made his peace with Pietro, realising that the reason he had clung so staunchly to his vow to the man who had been like a father to him was because he'd been convinced that it was the only reason Pietro had stayed close by. Pietro had told him that he was like a son to him, had offered his love freely, and let loose something in Santo he hadn't realised he'd been hiding. And that had finally given him the courage to come here tonight, for the one and only thing that could make him whole.

Mads and Kat made to leave and Santo took a deep

breath, slowly turning around to face the woman he
loved beyond distraction.

Eleanor.

Her steps almost faltered when she saw him turn. Almost, but not quite. Because she knew. She knew that he
was it for her. He was her family, her home, her heart, no
matter how much distance between them, or how much
time had passed. He had been that for her from the moment she'd first laid eyes on him, all those years ago.

She wasn't quite sure of the response she would get,
but she knew her love for him, she knew her own heart
and her own mind.

The guests parted before her, but she barely noticed.
Her gaze was on Santo, only Santo. She crossed the entire length of the ballroom while whispers grew louder
and, for the first time in her life, Eleanor truly didn't
care that she was under the scrutiny of the near two
hundred guests in attendance that evening—including
Edward Carson.

The man she had finally released herself from the
night before.

No, Freddie wasn't eighteen yet, and no, her mother
couldn't leave Edward Carson until that happened, but
Eleanor had finally stepped out from beneath his control and into her own light. A light that she desperately
wanted to share with Santo.

She didn't have much to offer him. Although her investments were good and her turnover impressive, her
bank balance was truly insignificant compared to the
people in this room. But she had enough to gain her

own independence. Enough to know that she could and would move forward with her life alone if she had to. And that knowledge, the knowledge that she could rely on herself to recover from whatever life threw at her, to get back up and stand on her own, had given her the confidence she'd needed to come here tonight and to confess her feelings for the man she loved.

'Santo,' she greeted him, her gaze hungrily consuming the sight of him.

He nodded, that muscle in his jaw flickering, warning her of his restraint. But she didn't want his restraint. She never had.

There was so much she wanted to tell him, so much that she could see in his eyes, but the most important of all was simply this.

'I love you,' she confessed with a shrug, as if she'd tried not to. As if she couldn't help it. As if she were sorry for herself, when she was none of those things.

'I...don't need you to love me back,' she said, her confidence wobbling, but not wavering. Because it was the truth. 'My love for you doesn't depend on a response. It's not a transaction, to be bought or sold, like so much here is. My love for you doesn't depend on what you choose to do or not do with it,' she confessed.

She'd learned that about herself and about what she wanted from life. That she had to be happy with her choices, her decisions, her feelings, first and foremost. And, no matter what happened, she needed Santo to know that she wasn't ashamed of her love for him and never would be.

She had been devastated that he had thought himself

unworthy of her. She had heard that in his tone when he'd accused her of being with him just to disappoint Edward. Seen through his accusation to the hurt that lay beneath. And she couldn't understand how he was unable to see that he was the best of every single person in this room.

'I just wanted you to know that. There will never be anyone else for me. There never was. It was always you,' she ended on a whisper.

Eleanor desperately imprinted the image of him on her memory in case it was all she would have in the months and years to come. Thick waves of dark hair making those aquamarine eyes even more hypnotic, lips almost cruelly carnal. She couldn't linger too long on any one feature because it was nearly too much for her to bear.

The silence in the room was deafening, not even a pin drop, not even the sound of her own heartbeat. Pressing her lips together to hide the way that they wobbled, she was about to turn, when suddenly he moved. And suddenly he was there. Everywhere. All at once.

His arms wrapped around her in that way of his that made her feel worshipped and loved and precious all at the same time. His lips found hers, not even trying to prise or entice them open to him, just to press against hers as if that was all he would ever need. She felt it, the passion, the love, the sheer magnitude of what she felt herself, returned to her by him. Her heart just gave itself to him and he accepted it.

'I didn't believe it. I couldn't trust that this was real, that you were real,' he whispered into her ear, holding her to him as if she might be snatched away from him at any minute. She felt his heart racing in his chest against her own. She felt the panic, the fear, the excitement, knew those same feelings *as* her own.

For a moment she couldn't believe it either, questioning whether it was real, whether she actually got to keep him this time.

'Can you ever forgive me?' The question exhaled from him as if it had been lodged in his chest for the entire year that they'd been apart.

She closed her eyes as the tears built, threatening to escape even as she wished them back.

'Can you ever forgive me?' she asked, unable to believe that she might have earned the right, having made him feel unworthy of her love.

The whispers and tittering of the people in the crowd began to grow, even as she would have been content to simply stay there, held by him, *loved* by him.

He pulled back to gaze into her eyes. And, just like that, the heat that had been banked behind declarations and confessions simmered into being.

'*Cristo*, Eleanor, I love you so damn much,' he said and she couldn't help the smile that split her heart apart and pulled it back together at exactly the same time— reformed by him, reformed *for* him. 'It's inconceivable to me that you don't already know. That you don't feel it. Because I can't feel anything else. At all. *All* I feel is my love for you. Nothing else matters. Not these people, not my company, not even the promise I made to Pietro. They are all insignificant in comparison to how much I love you.'

But before she could say anything he dropped to one knee as a gasp of shock echoed across the guests, filling the large ornate hall. Shivers racked her body as she realised that he was going to propose to her. It was more than she had dared let herself hope for in all the years she'd known that he was the one she wanted to spend her life with. And now that it was here her heart nearly exploded from the joy of it.

'Eleanor Carson—'

She shook her head so fast that it cut off his words. A second of doubt passed across his features before comprehension blocked it out completely. She hated that she'd put that there, but it was important to her that they got this right.

'It's Moretti,' she clarified, loudly and clearly. 'My name is Eleanor Moretti.'

Santo looked at Eleanor, the pride, the confidence shining from her as she declared herself Pietro's daughter. As she finally turned her back on the man who had caused more damage than any one man had a right to.

Things were falling into place in a way that he'd never dared hope for. He had asked for Pietro's approval just before flying out here, knowing that had Eleanor not come tonight, he would have searched the world for her.

And as she stood before him, beautiful beyond his comprehension, exquisite in scarlet, he held open his palm and lifted the lid on the box that his mother had given him. It wasn't her ring—that had been buried with the man who had never earned their love—but her mother's ring, his *nonna*'s.

The women of his family were some of the strongest people he knew, and Eleanor was no different. He loved her with a fierceness that would never weaken, and it was the bare minimum of what Eleanor deserved from her future.

From the corner of his eye, he saw Edward Carson throw back his drink and make a fuss leaving the room. He knew that Eleanor had seen it too, from the way that she stilled. Outwardly, no one would have seen her move, her gaze didn't falter from his, but Santo knew the courage that she'd needed to brave this and marvelled at how strong she had become.

'Eleanor Moretti,' he said loudly for the whole room to hear, 'would you do me the greatest honour of letting me love you, honour you and worship you for the rest of my days?'

'Only if you'll let me do the same,' she said with a smile that could have lit the world. The strength of her love felt like a wave of heat.

'Do you always have to argue with me?' he mock growled from the floor.

'I will be needing the last word in all arguments, yes,' she confirmed happily.

'Only if I get to kiss that word from your lips,' he replied, rising from his knee to his feet, his hands reaching for her as he drew to his full height, lifting her from the floor, her legs wrapping around him so that he could feel her all around him once again.

With his entire heart full, he leaned to whisper in her ear, 'Say yes. Please,' he all but begged. 'I just want to hear it.'

She turned her lips to his and replied, 'Yes. Yes, yes, yes, yes, yes,' she said, over and over again, and he would never tire of hearing it.

Mads and Kat led a round of applause that gained volume and strength throughout all the guests in attendance, aside from Tony Fairchild, who was as red as a beetroot, and Dilly Allencourt, who was practically green with envy.

Neither Santo nor Eleanor cared one bit. This would be the last time they ever attended a New Year's Eve event with these people, they knew it, and Santo marched from the grand ballroom with Eleanor still in his arms without a second look.

'Where are you taking me?' Eleanor asked him, laughter and happiness filling her in the way that only Santo could make it.

'Home,' Santo announced. He was taking her *home*.

EPILOGUE

New Year's Eve four years later, Puglia

SANTO WOULD NEVER grow tired of the sound of children's laughter. It pealed through the house and out on the wind, carried to him as he made his way home from the olive groves. There had been a time, in the not so distant past, when he would never have thought it possible to feel such a thing, knowing the promise he'd made to himself growing up with Gallo's fury. And now he was determined to fill his estate with as many different cries of joy, laughter and happiness as he could.

Since walking out of the Fouriers' party in Brussels four years ago, his life had changed considerably, and he didn't regret a single moment of it. Thankfully, the work he'd done to disengage himself from Edward Carson in the preceding years had significantly lessened the financial blows that fell.

But he was still hit hard. Some of the families had followed Carson's lead in wreaking their revenge, but a surprising number of them hadn't. And even more surprising was how quickly the group of twelve families had fractured and broken apart in the years following.

Some of the younger generation had little inclination for the cut-throat backstabbing that their forefathers had gone in for, and there had been an exodus as they followed Santo's suit.

The Sabatini Group had been forced to trim down operations in the wake of existing stakeholders' internal fighting. However, the resulting loss of their income had forced them to cut their losses or sell out. All of which was more than fine with Santo. It had simply meant that he could focus his business life on his venture with Mads Rassmussen and his personal life on Eleanor, on his relationship with his mother, with Pietro...with himself.

Santo had started that process four years ago and it hadn't been easy to work to rebuild some of the damage his father had done in his early years. Becoming a father himself had been the most incredible moment of his life, but also one of the hardest as he'd struggled to understand his father's actions and his complex feelings about his mother.

Eleanor had been there to support him every step of the way, but the help he'd needed went beyond her abilities. He'd started to see a counsellor for himself, but also for his children, wanting to make sure that he didn't repeat the pain of his childhood on them. And while it was one of the hardest things he'd ever done, every single minute he spent with his children showed him how much it was worth it—to make sure that they grew up with the kind of emotional strength and stability that he'd never had.

Eleanor had borne his emotional storms with a love and patience that astounded him and no one had cheered him on more as he'd created a charity for victims of domestic violence here in Puglia. He'd wanted her to be a part of it, but she was right, again, in that it was something that should be his alone.

He looked up at the light in the children's window and saw Eleanor's outline in the gauzy curtains billowing in the cool dusk breeze. She was getting them ready for the New Year's party that evening. He checked his watch; if he didn't get a move on he'd be late.

Santo cut through the garden and came into the villa by the back door, taking the stairs up to the second floor at a jog, stopping the moment he heard that sound again.

A fit of near hysterical giggles.

Only one thing caused that sound. His wife tickling their oldest. Little Pietro had inherited his mother's skin and sensitivity, but his father's humour and cheek. It was a lethal combination.

Their daughter Lucia had his eyes and from the first moment he'd looked on them he'd felt the erasure of pain when seeing his own reflection. His eyes were his daughter's, not his father's, and that meant more than he could ever hope to put into words. She had a mop of adorable blonde curls, but his mother informed him that they would eventually darken over time, just like they had with him. Personality-wise, though, she took very much after her mother and he adored her.

'Santo?' Eleanor called and he smiled to himself. She always knew when he was near.

'Sì?'

'Can you please convince your son that he needs to wear trousers for this evening?'

Santo came down the corridor to the bedroom opposite his and his wife's, and peered in with a frown.

'I'm not sure I can do that,' he said with grave seriousness.

'Oh, really? And why would that be, husband?' Eleanor asked with a raised eyebrow, but the glint in her eye told him that she knew there was mischief afoot.

'Because I don't think he *should* wear trousers this evening.'

Pietro jumped up and down, celebrating exuberantly.

'And if he's not wearing trousers this evening, then I don't need to wear trousers either,' Santo announced with a flourish.

Pietro stopped in an instant. 'No, Papà. You have to wear trousers!'

'But I can't leave you to be the only person not wearing trousers. So I'll keep you company by not wearing trousers.'

His gorgeous little boy frowned, trying to work through the complex reasoning of his desire to not wear trousers and his intense dislike of his father not doing so. It looked almost painful, and Santo tried very hard not to laugh.

'Papà wear my dress?' two-and-a-half-year-old Lucia offered in broken English.

'Oh, can I?' Santo asked with absolute delight.

'I'm not sure you'll fit,' Eleanor mused.

'I absolutely *will* fit,' Santo replied dramatically. 'Here, I'll show you.'

And both of his children descended into even more laughter as he toed off his shoe and tried to put his foot in Lucia's dress.

* * *

Eleanor didn't think she could love her husband any more than she did in that moment. This was everything she had never dared to dream that she could have.

It seemed incredible that she even wanted to celebrate New Year's Eve after the awfulness of the ten occasions she'd spent in different cities around Europe. But Santo had done that for her—healed parts of her that she'd never even known were damaged.

She still felt raw that he had suffered so much after the broken ties with the twelve families. She had grown up in business, become an adult in business. She knew the impact of the devastating loss and betrayal from such a large number of investors in the Sabatini Group.

Santo had done everything he could to reassure her that he was fine with reducing the company in the way he had been forced to do, and she believed him. It didn't stop her being angry for him though. And there had been quite a lot of anger for her to deal with in the months that had followed their escape.

Because that was what she'd seen it as. An escape. She had been imprisoned by lies and manipulation, and freedom had been quite an adjustment. But Santo had loved her through it all. Reassured her, soothed her, accepted her in every possible way.

It would have been so easy for him to dominate the relationship she had with Pietro, but he had encouraged her to find her own way with her biological father and it had meant everything to her. That he accepted the complexity of her feelings towards both her parents was huge for her. Parents who would, for the first time, be together under this roof tonight.

Much had changed in her mother's life, and Freddie's too. Analise had stayed with Edward until Freddie was eighteen years old and then moved out into a little flat, cutting all ties with her husband apart from communication via her lawyers. Freddie had gone with her and together they had weathered the storm of Edward's wrath.

Eleanor had begged them to come and stay with her and Santo, who would have welcomed them with open arms, but Analise and Freddie insisted that they wanted to handle it their way and she'd respected that. Freddie had grown into a man in so many ways since then. He was now at university and seeing a girl he'd met there, both of whom would also be coming tonight.

Santo's mother would also be joining them and bringing her companion. It had taken a while for Santo to warm to Enrico but the man had earned his grudging respect for the way that he treated his mother and she could tell that there was a sense of peace about Santo now that his mother had eventually found her own happiness. It was a peace that soothed many old hurts for her husband and, for that, she would be thankful for ever to Enrico.

'Right, you terrors, I'm going to leave you in your father's capable hands while I get myself ready. In my *own* dress. One that actually fits!' she cried, giving them all a last final kiss before getting into the shower.

Washed, scrubbed, moisturised and bright pink from the heat of the water, Eleanor wiped the steam away from the mirror. Wrapped in a towel and nothing else,

she thought she saw traces of the girl who had so op-
timistically entered the Hall of Antiquities in Munich
thirteen years ago. There were laughter lines at her eyes
now, knowing in her gaze, a few healed scars and a sense
of self she'd never have had without the journey she had
taken to be here.

And she'd change nothing. She loved the person she
was, the man she'd married and the children she'd born
with a passion and fervour she'd not known, let alone
thought herself capable of. What she had achieved with
Santo was a life, a home, a family that she was proud of.

Tears pressed against the backs of her eyes and she
waved her hand at them to stop them from falling. She
needed to put on her make-up and she couldn't get this
emotional yet.

'*Il mio cuore*, what's wrong?' Santo asked, stepping
into the bathroom behind her and wrapping her in his
arms.

'Oh, it's nothing. I'm just being silly,' she dismissed,
feeling the tears press even harder against her eyes. *Oh,
stupid hormones!* They were going to give it all away.
'I'm just so thankful for all that we have,' she said, holding his gaze in the reflection of the mirror.

His heart was in his eyes. She saw it every time he
looked at her, at their children. The love he gave them
was incredible.

'I never thought that I would feel this much love in
my life. You brought that to me, and there isn't a minute of a single day that I'm not thankful for it,' he said,
pulling her gently back against his chest.

Eleanor sighed, a small smile playing at her lips. She was never any good at keeping secrets anyway.

'Do you think there might be room for a little more?'

'A little more what?' he asked.

'A little more love to give. Because I have some news,' she confessed, turning in his arms and whispering that she was pregnant into his ear.

This time it was Santo's joy and laughter that could be heard from outside the villa as the Sabatini family members gathered to celebrate the happy news on New Year's Eve.

* * * * *

Were you swept up in the drama of
Forbidden Until Midnight?

Then why not try these other sensational stories
by Pippa Roscoe?

Expecting Her Enemy's Heir
His Jet-Set Nights with the Innocent
In Bed with Her Billionaire Bodyguard
Twin Consequences of That Night
Greek's Temporary 'I Do'

Available now!